Sin at Easter

J. Tumas-Vaižgantas savo dirbamajame kambaryje

VAIŽGANTAS

Juozas Tumas

Sin at Easter

and Other Stories

Translated from the Lithuanian by
DANGUOLĖ SEALEY, ALGIRDAS LANDSBERGIS,
STEPAS ZOBARSKAS, *and* CLARK MILLS

Biographical Outline by
ANTANAS VAIČIULAITIS

Edited by
NOLA M. ZOBARSKAS

Introduction by CHARLES ANGOFF

MANYLAND BOOKS • New York

PRINTED IN THE UNITED STATES OF AMERICA BY
Theo. Gaus' Sons, Inc., BROOKLYN, N. Y.

TABLE OF CONTENTS

INTRODUCTION

By Charles Angoff

THE DOMINANT EUROPEAN form of fiction writing, for a long
time, was opulent in both content and manner. It was also
leisurely, weaving in and out of a character, intertwining
observations about him with observations about those in
whose orbit he moves, and, equally important, indicating
what the land and environment contributed to his psyche.
Some of the opulent writers didn't hesitate to include philosophical comments on the passing scene and on broad
philosophical issues. Thomas Mann's *The Magic Mountain*
is a rich repository of medical knowledge, geographical
learning, and psychological speculation, as well as a fasci-
nating narrative. The same is true of the novels of Ladislas
Reymont and Sigrid Undset and Selma Lagerlöff—and, of
course, Tolstoy and Dostoevsky, in a way, the fathers of the
whole opulent movement. These masters reflected eras as
well as portrayed men and women. Their writings are vast
canvases of a time and place, with individuals highlighting
the qualities of both time and place.

American literature, at the time of the New England
Golden Age and for the first two decades of the present
century, was clearly influenced by the aforementioned aspect
of European literature. Melville comes to mind at once.
Moby Dick is European in its sweep and highflown meta-
physical meditations. Hawthorne was a little less so. Henry
James was clearly in the European tradition. There were no
such things to him as passing moments; they were all preg-

vii

nant with significance, which he set about detailing in many pages. Then there were Theodore Dreiser and Thomas Wolfe and John Steinbeck. The present-day mood in American fiction finds this alien, but there are already signs that the reading public is yearning for the old manner, for it is realizing that illumination of character and time is preferable to the superficial enjoyment of a swift-moving narrative, and it is illumination that the world today is much in need of.

Father Vaižgantas belongs to the grand old school of leisurely, illuminating writers of fiction. Along with all writers of stature he can glorify the commonplace, cast so much compassion and understanding about his characters that one surrenders petty moral judgment and is entranced by the complexities and miracles and bewilderments that God hath wrought. To Father Vaižgantas there are no mere good people and mere bad people. There are only people, some of whom get lost in this world of greed and malice and pointless competition—and in their bewilderment do things that, at times, seem to be done by creatures far removed from them. Father Vaižgantas seems to say that what the good Lord thought enough of to create is sufficient for us just to contemplate, always with pity, never with rancor.

The longest story in this collection, "Sin at Easter"— it is really a novella—features Vaižgantas' method and basic qualities probably at their best. Two young men, Jonas and Kazys, come to no good end because of a girl, Anelja, who marries one of them, though she is in love with the other, who returns her love. A situation of tabloid banality, but the author brings a whole period in Lithuanian history to life, and he does it in terms of simple people, in whom he sees glory as well as pathetic helplessness.

There is a subsidiary character—in a sense she is, so to speak, the backbone of the story—who is one of the most arresting women in modern European fiction. Her name is Aunt Apolonija, a midwife to whom, apparently, delivering a child is a spiritual duty and delight. "She had such a gentle hand that not one of the newly born babies had to cry in distress." Though sixty years old she has immense charm and appeal to young men, and Kazys obviously is deeply in love with her. She is not unmindful of his attachment and she handles him with aplomb. Indeed, she sets the tone of the small community, in many respects, and what goes on in her home reflects what is happening in the village of Puzionys. Her smile is a benediction; her hesitation is an admonition. She is the Eternal Woman.

"Aleksiukas' Father and Mother" is little more, on the surface, than a double sketch of two parents and their son. The mother is quite a talker. "She was silent only when she slept." Her husband is the silent one, who seems to be devoid of most of the masculine "privileges": "He had never learned to swear, and anyone who had the misfortune to provoke him, heard no stronger word than 'rascal.' " Then, "he was equally unable to rejoice aloud." He looked to his wife for advice, encouragement, for nearly everything. But the son saw the loveliness in his silent father and was deeply attached to him. "His father's glance made Aleksiukas tremble with happiness." That's about all there is to the tale except for an episode involving the search for an apple. A brief sketch, but rich with tenderness, and the reader will long remember it.

The other two stories, "Rimas and Nerimas" and "The Misfit" are worthy, too. Especially is this true of the first. It begins simply, "Rimas and Nerimas, two farmers from Augštaičiai, lived across from one another at the very end of the village." What one did the other also did, almost by what seemed predestination. Then fate intervened, there was a rift in friendship, the rift was patched up—but, really, not quite. Life resumed its old routine, now with a little pain adding a bit of unpleasantness into what had been so good. A slice of life this story is, but told with such commiserating objectivity that one is left aghast at the ways of fate.

Father Vaižgantas deserves to be better known in America. He is a man of enormous skill and great heart, an ideal combination for an artist of stature. There are not many writers of the past half century who have so much to say in fiction and who say it so beautifully.

CHARLES ANGOFF
*Fairleigh Dickinson
University*

Rutherford, New Jersey

VAIŽGANTAS
(1869-1933)

By Antanas Vaičiulaitis

VAIŽGANTAS, whose real name was Juozas Tumas, was born in the county of Svėdasai on September 8, 1869, the feast of the Nativity of Our Lady. In keeping with the day his devout mother offered the infant to the service of God. The boy grew up on a farm in a large family. Although sickly in his early years, he was lively in character and sensitive to nature, which held for him a mystical appeal. During the formative years of his youth he developed an optimistic outlook and acquired an immense treasure of linguistic and ethnographic lore. After graduating from high school, he entered the seminary in Kaunas in 1889 and was ordained in 1893. In time he became one of the trio of Lithuanian priests who gained fame for their contributions to Lithuanian literature, the others being the poet Maironis and the critic and scholar, Adomas Jakštas—Dambrauskas. During the period of Lithuanian independence they were neighbors, all living in the vicinity of the City Hall Square in Kaunas.

From an early age Vaižgantas devoted himself to the service of Lithuanian letters. His first published article appeared in 1889; it was a report on local activities. But his journalistic work was interrupted for a few years because of illness. In 1896 he became editor of the Catholic periodical *Tėvynės Sargas* (Guardian of the Homeland) and he served in this capacity for six years. This was a dangerous task because the printing of Lithuanian books and periodicals was forbidden by the Russians since 1864. The ban was rescinded only after forty years of conflict. Lithuanian printing was done mostly in East Prussia and then smuggled across the border into Lithuania. Those caught were sentenced to hard labor and exiled to Siberia. This was one of the reasons why the young and restless priest had to be sent from one parish to another. His first assignment was in Jelgava, Latvia, where he met among others Jonas Jablonskis, the linguist who standardized the modern Lithuanian language, and the jurist Antanas Kriščiukaitis, who under the pen-name of Aišbė wrote some realistic stories of Lithuanian country life. In Jelgava Vaižgantas himself began writing his *Aukštaičių Vaizdeliai* (Highland Sketches), consisting of his childhood reminiscences. Later these recollections were woven into his most ambitious work of fiction, *Pragiedruliai* (Sunbeams). However, for the time being his literary work was mostly of a journalistic nature. When the ban on Lithuanian printing was lifted in 1904, his energy found its outlet in political activities for achieving greater national freedom in Lithuania. Together with the future president of Lithuania, Antanas Smetona, he established a new magazine, *Viltis* (Hope), in Vilnius, and was one of the main contributors to it from 1907 to 1910. In 1911 he visited the United States to raise funds for *Saulės Namai* (House of the Sun, the headquarters of a Catholic educational association). He told his impressions of America in his book, *Ten gera, kur mūsų, nėra* (It is good where we are not).

The First World War found him in Riga, Latvia, where he took care of refugees from Lithuania and occupied himself increasingly with writing fiction. In 1917 he took an active part in the St. Petersburg Lithuanian Conference, where he spoke for the independence of Lithuania. In the same year he traveled to Stockholm as a delegate to another Lithuanian conference. There he found such prominent Lithuanian writers as Ignas Šeinius* and Vincas Mykolaitis—Putinas. He immersed himself in writing *Pragiedruliai*. The first volume of it was published in Vilnius in 1918, the year when Lithuania regained her independence. Now Vaižgantas began the most creative period of his life. Besides continuing *Pragiedruliai*, he wrote what is perhaps his most beautiful book, *Dėdės ir Dėdienės* (Uncles and Aunts), and the narrative *Nebylys*, which in this collection is named "Sin at Easter." Another moving story from this period is *Išgama* ("The Misfit"). With the earlier "Rimas and Nerimas," these three narratives constitute the zenith of his shorter fiction.

At the same time he was rector of the historic Vytautas Church in Kaunas, lecturer on contemporary Lithuanian literature at the University of Lithuania in Kaunas, president of the Lithuanian Writers Association, and a member of numerous other organizations, in addition to his editorial work.

Because of the sheer radiance of his personality, the goodness of his heart, his unquenchable optimism, and the golden tone of his spoken word, and despite some misunderstandings with his lay associates and spiritual superiors, Vaižgantas was the most beloved postwar personality in all Lithuania, both among peasants and intellectuals. This was due even more to his inner warmth than to his writings.

To add a personal note, as a teenager I traveled from my village some seventy kilometers to Kaunas mainly to see and hear Vaižgantas. To this day I treasure the moment when I saw him, white-haired, blue-eyed and radiant, as he went to church to say Mass and preach. It is said that even Jews used to come occasionally to listen to the preaching of the silver-tongued Vaižgantas.

At the end of his fruitful years and after his many strenuous efforts for his country, he could rightly state: "I

---

* His novel *Rejuvenation of Siegfried Immerselbe* was published by Manyland Books in 1965.

xiii

became the servant of my Lithuanian flock; no, even more, its slave." He died on April 29, 1933 in Kaunas and is buried in the Basilica of that city, not far from Bishop Valančius (1801-1875), who was the first to begin publishing Lithuanian books in East Prussia during the years of the press ban, and his neighbors from the City Hall Square, Maironis and Adomas Jakštas—Dambrauskas.

Vaižgantas was one of the most prolific of Lithuanian authors. The first four volumes of his *Collected Works* (*Vaižganto Raštai*) comprise his journalistic writings. Apart from these there are his studies of Lithuanian literature. The largest volume in this group is his book on Maironis. Finally, as a creative writer, he has achieved the status of a classic.

His first attempts at imaginative writing were some short comedies, but this was not his field. His largest work is the three-volume novel, *Pragiedruliai* (Sunbeams, 1918 and 1920), a vast panorama of Lithuania at the end of the nineteenth century and the beginning of the twentieth. Vaižgantas himself called this book *Pictures in the Cultural Struggle*. In these volumes he brings to light two characteristics of the Lithuanian outlook: the tendency to mysticism and romanticism on the one hand, and down-to-earth practicality accompanied by a certain degree of stubbornness on the other. He presents the reader with a whole gallery of colorful characters and revives the customs and the toil of earlier days. He was especially successful in recapturing the mysteries of his native landscape. The present collection includes "Aleksiukas' Father and Mother" from *Pragiedruliai*, depicting his parents. In these excerpts the reader has a glimpse of the mystic side of the characters, as he listens to the mother praying to the earth: "At night, when she gave thanks for the blessings of the day, she would fall prostrate on the ground, embracing it and kissing it devoutly, and address herself directly to the earth: 'Black Earth, Holy Earth, I humbly kiss thee, I thank thee, I thank thee for bearing me, sustaining me, and giving me joy . . .' "

Pragiedruliai at its best reaches the peaks of Lithuanian fiction. But the book suffers from being loosely knit and prone to digressions. Providing a clear and vivid picture of Lithuania some eighty years ago, *Pragiedruliai,* as observed by the poet and professor of literature, Vincas Mykolaitis—Putinas, "gives such a broad representation that it is impossible to find its equal in any other book of our literature."

Among the best and most charming books in Lithuanian letters is Vaižgantas' *Dėdės ir Dėdienės* (Uncles and Aunts, 1920-21), dealing with the last years of serfdom in Lithuania. It is a compact book telling a story of unfulfilled love. The action takes place in the open fields, and Vaižgantas is unsurpassed in his descriptions of peasants' toils, sufferings and longings, and of their life in the bosom of rustic nature. With the already mentioned narratives *Rimai ir Nerimai* (1915), *Išgama* (1929) and *Nebylys* (1930), this book constitutes the crown of Vaižgantas' artistic achievement.

Antanas Vaičiulaitis

Sin at Easter

Sin at Easter

Translated by Danguolė Sealey

THE SILENT MAN

PERHAPS I HAVE ALREADY mentioned the occasion when, in a remote part of Lithuania, I was asked to administer the last rites to a beggar of unusual character. He appeared from time to time in the district and astonished everyone by his complete disregard for what went on around him. Or, to be more precise, he refused to look at anything at all, whether it was close to him or at a distance; on the ground, in the sky, or situated on the horizon. Although his eyes were clear, they were at the same time clouded as if by a mist. He understood what was said to him and listened when he was told to, but he made not the slightest effort to reply. He was like a block of ice in cold weather, pierced through and through by sun rays which are not strong enough to melt it.

He ate whatever he was given, although he never asked for food or thanked the folks who fed him. He would enter a cottage, as if to take a rest; and there he would sit awhile, lost in thought, without seeming to notice anything. And if, during that short interval, he was not offered refreshment, he would get up and go out without a word. Exactly the same thing would happen in the next cottage. Bread he devoured like some elephant, without seeming to savor it or appearing to notice whether he was eating one slice or two. For all intents and purposes, he might just as well have been

1

chewing on the sole of an old shoe. He displayed an appetite only when a large bowl of soup was placed on the table before him. This he savoured as though it were a delicacy which he had not tasted for a long, long time. But even then he didn't seem to know or care whether it was borscht or cabbage or barley or potato soup that he was eating. If his hosts showed any inclination to talk to him while he ate and grew impatient when they received no reply, the old man would simply get up and, leaving the food which he obviously needed so badly, go elsewhere.

A man is likely to show displeasure when he is asked to give alms, but who will give without being asked? To be offered a bowl of soup was indeed a rare luxury for the old man, who lived almost entirely on dry bread and water which he drank when he was outside. He would never look for a bucket of water or a tin cup while he was indoors. He was a worn-out old man, nothing but bones in a bag of skin.

Nobody knew who he was or where he came from, neither the village people nor the police, and nobody paid much attention to him. But one day, the family which was feeding him noticed that he was too weak to arise from the bench. He just sat there, leaning against the wall, until they put him to bed. Then the master of the cottage hitched up the horses and sent for the priest, who, in this case, happened to be myself.

When I was left alone with the beggar, I couldn't get a single word out of him. I asked him to cross himself, but he refused to do so. He simply stared straight ahead as though he were stricken with palsy. Neither his lips nor any other muscle in his face moved. His cheeks were emaciated and his forehead was so wrinkled that I scarcely believed so many deep furrows could exist in so narrow a space. I began to count them and counted up to fifteen without including the fine lines at the temples. It was obvious that the beggar had been exhausted by starvation.

Suddenly, I grew ashamed for having wasted so much

time. Hastily kneeling at the old man's bedside, I began to recite the ritual prayers loudly in Lithuanian, with my eye on the Latin text. Then, all at once, I heard what sounded like some cockroach rustling along a crack in the wall. Rising quickly to my feet, I put my ear to the sick man's lips and made out his words with great difficulty.

". . . I desecrated the Feast of Easter, the very Resurrection. . . . I killed a friend, I killed my mother. Lord, Lord, why don't you take away the burden from me. . . . It is exactly 30 years now. . . ."

I brightened up at once and began to feel as pleased as if I had won a lottery. Taking the face of the unhappy man in my hands, I kissed his wrinkles from the depth of my heart. Then I said to him:

"*Pax tecum!* The Lord is taking your burden away. He is taking it away. I forgive you all your sins in the name of the Father. . . . You may have done much wrong, but you have certainly suffered enough for it. . . ."

By the time I had finished speaking, he was dead.

It was difficult for me even to imagine such a tragedy. How overwhelming and sudden must have been the deed to have stunned the doer for thirty years. Nor could I hope to discover how it had happened, for the dead man had spoken in a dialect which was foreign to the district, even though it was not unfamiliar to me. I was dumbfounded.

Many years went by, and then one day I found myself visiting the locality where this very same dialect was spoken. I had relatives and friends there, and when they had gathered together of an evening and after we had eaten a little and quaffed some beer, I began to press the older ones for stories about their district.

"Oh, yes! There are certainly plenty of stories to tell." And very soon the old folks began to regale us with accounts of strange happenings, of practical jokes that had been played, and of terrible, hair-raising crimes.

One story seemed somewhat familiar to me. Had I heard something like it before? Or even seen . . . ? I listened attentively to the narrator. Fifty years ago, perhaps even longer, an ordinary, insignificant village suddenly gained notoriety because of a cruel and senseless act of manslaughter committed there—an act which also resulted in the destruction of two homesteads. Suddenly, I remembered the beggar whom I had assisted in his final hour. I added what I heard to what the dying man had whispered to me twenty years ago, and reconstructed the following picture.

You are free to believe it or not, just as you wish.

AUNTY

MOST OF THE INHABITANTS of the village of Puzionys had been brought into the world by Mrs. Apolonija Butkys—or Aunty as everyone there called her. No other name was used, even though in other villages of the district the midwife was always referred to as "grandma."

She had learned the art of midwifery from the woman who had assisted at the birth of her own children; and in developing special skills, she drew on her own experience. She had such a gentle hand that not one of the newly born babies had to cry in distress, much less depart from this world on arrival. Nor had she ever infected the blood of a child-bearing woman and given her fever. It was fortunate for the Puzionys village to have such a wonderful midwife at hand. In these matters, at least, there was no cause for alarm; there were none of the long illnesses, for which farmers' wives had little time. Most important of all, the villagers were spared the unnecessary expenses and disappointments which bring many a gray hair to the heads of parents. The villagers never had to call in the professional midwife who, however indispensable elsewhere, was for some reason never popular. And it is true that, as a rule, she proved to be a most unattractive woman who would eat like a horse while doing nothing, apparently intent on consuming enough food to last for the rest of her life. She would also stay on for two or three weeks at a stretch, upsetting the household and getting underfoot like some unnecessary and cumbersome piece of furniture.

"And what a blessing it is to have such help at confinements," the villagers of Puzionys would boast to their neighbors whenever they happened to meet and sit down for a chat over drinks. "As for her presence, we scarcely feel it. She appears suddenly, like a stork, puts down what she has found and goes away again cheerfully."

Together with each safely delivered child, a new happiness remained in the cottage for awhile, as if Aunty's presence was that of a guardian angel who had come to visit his charges in a dream. Apolonija came, accomplished her task without getting in anybody's way or being a nuisance to anyone, and was gone.

The whole district envied the good fortune of Puzionys. From time to time, they would try to entice Aunty away with costly gifts, but nothing ever came of it.

"Oh no, no, my good man, I couldn't possibly come with you," she would say to some would-be client. "I only know how to help my own women. . . . I do for them what I can." And the poor man would have no heart to keep insisting.

"There you are! What did I say. She won't come and that's that! Such a clever midwife!"

In nearly all the villages of Upper Lithuania, the houses face each other in pairs on either side of the street. Directly opposite the Butkys family house stood the house of a family named Šnerva. These two families could hide nothing from each other and could follow each other's movements with ease. Indeed, they did not attempt to hide anything since there was nothing really to hide. Only Apolonija, when she was getting ready for a "mission," carried out her preparations secretly, without perhaps knowing herself why she did so.

It would have been scarcely possible for the Šnervas not to notice whenever some village man who was otherwise seldom seen at their end of the street came striding intently across the Butkys yard. Everyone knew that the stork was

5

already circling above such an individual's chimney. The man usually spent a long time on the porch or in the small corridor wiping the mud from his shoes or from his best wooden clogs, for in rainy weather the mud in Lithuanian village streets can rise to one's very ankles. He would stand there, pounding his feet against the floor boards so noisily that he could be heard three houses away, yet he would still hesitate to go inside. All at once he would feel the need to blow his nose or to cough and clear his throat; until, before he knew it, the door latch was lifted and there stood Aunty herself. It was easy to follow their conversation from the Šnerva yard.

"Why do you stand there, stamping around for a whole hour like a horse? Don't you know how to open the door? Well, it's time, is it then?" Aunty would say sternly, but with such a pleasant voice that the caller's moustache, trimmed to a small brush, would vanish completely between his nose and his smiling lips.

"Oh, it is indeed time, Aunty! She's screaming her head off; the pains are hemming her in," the caller would reply, removing his fur cap politely from his head which was as round as a bludgeon, and bending low to kiss her hand.

The visitor expressed as best he could, with his whole bearing and with his face and voice, the affection, respect and boundless trust he felt for the woman who stood before him. He turned to her as a drowning man turns to the only person who can save him.

To Apolonija, however, neither his appearance on her doorstep nor his words and anxiety for his wife were anything new. She knew, in advance, where and by whom she would be needed and in what words the request would be framed. She had heard a hundred times before the solemn seriousness of the husband, already the father of many children, presenting his case; and the nervous, desperate manner of a young married man expecting his firstborn. Even though the young man himself was not confined to bed or exposed to birth pains and danger, he evidently shared in the suffer-

6

ing of his wife and trembled with fear, praying to God that all would be well with her.

"Don't you worry, now. You'll see, everything will turn out well. It's nothing new. God intended it to be this way for womenfolk. How else could it be?" Apolonija would proceed to soothe the anxious, frightened soul.

She then broke off her work at once, no matter how urgent the task. She did not permit anything to detain her. If she was interrupted when her oven was well heated and ready for the pots to be set on the fire, she would summon the first person available, whether man or woman, and leave them to carry on with her work. There was no doubt about it, she had her family well trained. One had to marvel at the devotion of this well-to-do farmer's wife to a duty which she had taken upon herself out of sheer good will.

Since she was always neat and presentable, Apolonija did not take long to get herself ready. She was not ashamed to go out just as she was. All she had to do was take the surgical instruments out of the chest and unfold her large woolen Sunday shawl. In winter and in summer both, she would wrap herself up in this shawl before setting forth on her "mission," more as a matter of ritual than need: just as a Jew puts on his colored scarf or tallith when he makes ready to pray.

The delivery of an infant into the world was a sacred task to Apolonija; it was a work to be accomplished in prayer, so to speak. This was the way she increased the Lord's worshipers. In this way she took part and was present at the most important family celebration and the deepest mystery of nature. At such times she was like an extended part of nature, a note that cannot be crossed out from a melody, not merely a person who invaded another household for her own purposes. She personified the very force of Christianity and of the nation. She felt that she must express these feelings outwardly by wearing her shawl, a single festive piece of clothing in which she herself was shrouded like a mystery.

7

"There she goes! He's fetching her away," the neighbors would whisper to each other excitedly while watching them through the windows. The man, though usually sure-footed, walked on ahead unsteadily with his head bent, as if ploughing the ground with his eyes. He did not notice the unevenness of the path, which caused him to stumble again and again. At this hour his sole concern was for his wife, for the one person who had to suffer now and writhe in pain, all alone, all by herself because of something that a little while before had been their whim. How well the neighbors understood his feelings; how they longed to sympathize with him and wish him well, with their hearts if not with words. They felt somewhat reassured on seeing Aunty following close after him.

A short, sturdy little person, she walked behind the visitor wrapped so well in her shawl that an onlooker might wonder how she could possibly manage to see where she was going. The very fact that she had taken the trouble to mask herself from inquisitive eyes made the nature of her errand clear to everyone. Beneath her shawl, in her hands crossed firmly across her breast, she carried her husband's razor, like a conspirator about to stab his enemy in the heart. She hastened along the street—mystery personified about to confront another mystery: that which as yet was not, but soon would be; as yet unknown, but rich in potentialities.

Apolonija had trained the whole village as well as she had trained her own household. After all, she was a woman who bore on her head and shoulders the responsibility for their farm and a little while earlier for small children, as well as for the rest of her household. She could not afford to spend long hours away from home with sick people. It was her custom to instruct the pregnant women well beforehand how to take care of themselves and what preparations to make for their important day. So, at the house where she was expected, hot water was always at hand and on the corner of the table, refreshments were set out for her. There was a jug of warmed beer topped with cream, and a dish full of butter, among other things. In the pocket of the infant's father, five golden coins had been set aside for her and near the mother's bed, more gifts awaited her such as a linen guest towel, woven in squares, a woman's waist band and sometimes even an embroidered tablecloth. All was according to the householder's pocket, of course. When she had bathed the little newcomer, wrapped him up well and made the sign of the cross over him, thus entrusting the child with full confidence to Providence, Aunty sat down to eat at the end of the table. She talked gaily while she ate but soon rose and, wishing God's blessing on everyone, returned home to her interrupted work.

On her way home, she was an entirely different person; she walked along with a clear countenance, carrying on her left arm the shawl, beautifully folded because she needed it no longer. Everything was in the open now and there was no more need for secrecy. Now was the time for rejoicing, a time for pride, a time to prepare for the Christening. Since she had not caused any harm to anyone, Apolonija returned home pleased with herself and at peace. The neighbors were quick to understand her mood and said to one another:

"It's all over, thank God! She has a fine hand! May He grant her health and a long life."

Aunty had a fine hand, it is true, but she was careful and did not leave anything to chance. Her surgical instruments shone like silver; she always kept them meticulously clean. On the first occasion that Aunty had mustered enough courage to serve as midwife, she took her husband's razor along with her and she had kept it ever since. When the razor was not in use, she wrapped it up neatly in white paper and stored it in a chest.

"Go and buy yourself another. This razor is not for shaving the beard anymore," she told her husband firmly, and he did not dream of arguing with her. He went about unshaven for a day or two and then bought himself another razor.

9

In this uncomplicated manner, Apolonija came to terms with the complicated process of birth. Although she nursed the women of Puzionys more out of good will than necessity, the practice of midwifery brought its own benefits. Thanks to her skill, she was able to earn her maid's wages and contribute to the welfare of her family in other ways. Her chests were full of linen so that her household washing needed not to be done during the cold winter months on days when other women were forced to splash about in the ice holes. None of her family ever wore torn or patched clothes. There were only the hired man's wages to be paid in cash and the taxes on the land to be set aside.

At home, Apolonija was a cherished and irreplaceable member of the family. She was always busy, always concerned about one thing or another. Like a worker-bee who carries pale wax or sweet honey into the hive, she was constantly cheerful and jolly.

Aunty was certainly a blessing to her house and to her village. At home she was obeyed as if she were a queen-bee, while in the village she was respected like a sergeant-major. This was not done in any cold or calculating way; it was because she was so good and useful to everyone. In her relations with people, Aunty did not particularly try to please. She was like the sun which cannot help but shine brightly, or the orchard with flowers full of fragrance in May. In such matters, there is no room for thought or speculation. Such things have to be felt and the less they are thought about, the better.

Apolonija was not young. She was sixty years old. But her womanliness was still very much apparent. She was as kind and affectionate as ever, and surely kindness covers up many shortcomings.

Although Apolonija's looks had already faded, her face was not wrinkled. It was marked by only two deep lines, the so-called laughter lines around the mouth, which resulted from an almost perpetual smile. It was not entirely absent even when she slept.

Likeable features are not acquired at will. An assumed expression of kindness will of necessity be seen through straight away since it does not reflect the inward disposition. If only a person were to spend a great deal of time watching flowers grow or paying attention to bees when they are ready to swarm, what lovely features he would acquire! The countenance of the angriest woman would surely change for the better were she to observe, for long periods of time, children of angelic character. Happy the man or woman who is the owner of likeable features. They reveal much about the state of the soul.

A person who wears a mask, who appears to be that which he is not, at least for short periods of time, repulses others who have no need to do likewise. A child who knows nothing of physiognomy, who perhaps scarcely troubles to look at a face, is able to tell at once if the affection shown towards him is genuine. If it is not, he will refuse to have anything to do with such a person and will cry when he is fondled, as if such contact brought him bodily pain. A child's instincts are usually right. A person to whom he stretches out his arms, eager to embrace and kiss him, a person with whom a child is content to stay, deserves to be trusted and loved. Whoever despises such a person and shuns him is most likely a scoundrel and certainly a man of a different world.

Perhaps Kazys Šnerva from across the street still possessed the innocent instincts of a child, because his love for Aunty was as strong as ever. It was a pity that he did not dare to behave like a child any more. He had already entered into his fourth decade and did not think that a display of affection was fitting at his age.

If only Kazys had known how foolish he was in refusing expression to feelings which change earth into heaven! By holding himself back, by refusing to show his love, he was castrating himself; he was making himself an eunuch at heart.

Admittedly, there are different kinds of love. We are not talking here about a young man's love for his sweetheart or his fiancée; at certain times, certain things are permissible and at others they are not. But even so, his love for a wife or sweetheart does not interfere with the love a young man feels for his mother. Surely, both kinds of love bring happiness. This is perhaps especially true of the love felt for a mother, which is the more spiritual of the two kinds of love. Anyone who does not understand this is an ox or a blockhead. But a man who knows this, and holds back his feelings on purpose, does harm to himself quite unnecessarily.

Kazys had felt a strong liking for Aunty all along, for thirty years to be more precise. He had liked her when he was a little boy and was known to everyone as Kaziukas. Later, when he grew up to be Kazys, or to give him his full title, Kazimieras Šnerva, his feelings remained unchanged. He felt more drawn to her than even to his own mother.

When he was small, Kaziukas would run to Aunty with his arms outstretched, embrace her legs and press his face against her thigh. Or, he would clamber unceremoniously into her lap and curl up beside her own son, Joniukas. But now, Kazys had to be content with watching the object of his affection from afar, scarcely daring to kiss the old woman's hand.

Oh foolish, foolish Kazys! When you've kissed her hand, embrace your Aunty, just as you used to do. Kiss her lips and her neck! Let her old heart feel the beating of your young one! For such happiness, there is no price on this earth; it is the very gift of heaven. To take pleasure in your Aunty's presence from afar is all very well, but remember that the reflection of the sun does not equal the sun itself.

Apolonija knew that her son Jonas loved her and that his friend Kazys cared for her perhaps no less. Whenever she spoke to him or he to her, Kazys shone like the sun and behaved as though he was unaware of the rest of the world around him. If Aunty happened to be at home when he called on the Butkyses, he would want to remain there for hours and feel no desire to go back to his own house.

Jonas and Kazys were the same age and had been inseparable ever since childhood. When they were very little, they used to sit in some out-of-the-way sunny spot in the spring and make mud pies. In the summer they launched their wooden toy boats in the river. When they grew older, they herded cattle together; and when they were fully grown they labored in adjoining fields. They were firm friends, such as are seldom found. Not once had there been a disagreement between them to mar their relationship so that it had to be glued together again like a broken pot. Their friendship was happy, firm and steadfast. Usually, such a friendship is to be found only among people who live some distance from each other and who do not get under one another's feet all the time so that it becomes easy to take each other for granted.

Although there were other young lads of the same age in Puzionys, only Jonas and Kazys were so close. People teased them about it; they said that the lads were like two kernels under one shell.

Apolonija could rest assured as to the safety of her little son when he was with Kazys. In time she grew so accustomed to seeing the two boys together that she made no distinction between them at mealtimes or when she presented them with small gifts. In truth, one could not fail to love Kazys who was a good, affectionate, and well-mannered lad. Had anyone asked Apolonija which of the two boys she would have pitied more if a mishap had befallen either of them, she would have answered, as any true mother would, that all fingers hurt no matter which one of them is injured.

All the village people loved Apolonija. It was not surprising, after all, that she was popular with the men. But the women liked her, too, even the gossips who had nothing good to say for anyone else. Aunty was perhaps the only person in Puzionys about whom not a single bad word was ever spoken. Partly it was because the women scarcely considered her a threat to the menfolk they loved.

Apolonija was pleasant to see and to hear. The people of Puzionys liked to have in their village at least one woman who, although not tall in stature and by no means young, had nevertheless an ample figure, plump and well-rounded. Aunty was certainly not a thin woman, or dry as a withered branch: a person to make you think at once of scanty living and slender means. Neither was she flat as a herring because of a poor figure. Yet, although she was ample and well-rounded, she was not fat and shapeless; she had not ruined her looks through self indulgence. Her plumpness was of an appealing kind and did not prevent her from moving about quickly as she looked after her household and took care of the animals. She was the recipient of the kind of reverance that people bestow on those they look up to, whether they like to or not: such as the poor, for instance, bestow on the rich, the hired hands on the farmers, and the common folk on the village elders.

Apolonija was held in high esteem by her neighbors because she was not proud or given to boasting, although she had much to boast about. She knew, however, how to rejoice from the heart with a neighbor at his good fortune. She never complained about being tired or having too much to do. She was not like a hen who cackles loudly when she has laid an ordinary egg. People, as a rule, are not fools; they are well able to judge another's true value, and boasting only harms the boaster.

Aunty was also very hospitable and generous. No child was ever sent away from her door without an apple or a piece of cake in his hand; and she would most certainly not allow anyone to leave her house without making him sit at table, or at least offering him a drink.

The list of virtues could go on forever. As it is, I fear I might have praised her too much already. But people like Aunty are few, and they deserve full praise.

THE PEOPLE OF PUZIONYS

THE PEOPLE OF PUZIONYS were eastern Highlanders. The following description, written in 1861 by old Father Alekna, the rector of Merkine, could just as easily apply to them. "The character of the Lithuanian peasants, their disposition, their understanding of the world around them, and their evaluation of the past are naive, gay and derisive. At all times and everywhere, during their leisure hours or when they are hard at work in the fields; engaged in conversation within the family circle or taking part in some large gathering, there is always plenty of laughter, joking and merriment among them. They have at their command a goodly number of nicknames, are quick to make fun of others, and do not mind, in the least, if others make fun of them."

In other words, they were good-hearted people, of a pleasant disposition, and fully contented with their own far-from-luxurious way of life. Long years of Polish and Russian suppression had inhibited their development, so that even now they displayed no tendencies towards liveliness or unrest. The farm implements and the household utensils which they used had remained unchanged for the last five hundred years. Their wagons and harnesses, which were fashioned out of wood and rope, were adequate for the small loads they carried and for their short journeys. A nearby country town supplied them with all kinds of small necessities, while their clothing and linen were made at home.

When the young men married, they chose wives from among the village girls, whom they had known since childhood. It was almost unheard of for a man to marry a girl from another parish. Consequently, nearly all the inhabitants of the village were related to one another. There were brothers-in-law and sisters-in-law or, at the very least, godfathers and godmothers. The children lived just as their parents had done before them, in cottages with little windows and fireplaces without chimneys; and they wore clothes made of rough, homespun cloth. They had very little milk, even for their own consumption, although there were vast marshlands in the valley nearby, which would have provided ideal pastures had they been drained. The villagers observed Lent very strictly, abstaining from milk

15

and fat altogether—perhaps because the supply of these products was very scant at this time of the year.

Among all the eastern Highlanders, the people of the Puzionys village were the least spoken about. They were settled in their ways and they were the quietest of a quiet lot. The young people of the village did not strive after higher education; they did not show off at holiday time in city-made jackets decorated with white or yellow buttons; they did not return to their village sporting gaudy uniforms or caps decorated with stars. They were not in the habit of taking anyone to court. The common boundaries which they shared with their neighbors were broad and clearly marked, and there were no large estates at all in the neighborhood. The menfolk of Puzionys were of a peaceable character; they did not cause disturbances or pick fights in taverns.

Coming home with a bloody forehead was always considered improper, but it was exactly the way young men from other villages tried to prove their manliness to their womenfolk. This at least enlivened somewhat a way of life which must have seemed very monotonous and boring to an outsider.

No one from the village of Puzionys had ever emigrated to America to make his fortune. The village people would have found it difficult to grasp that there were other ways of making one's living in the world than farming. They could not conceive of urban industry, where a great deal of money could be earned and then spent in buying many unnecessary or superfluous things.

The people did not even know how to pronounce the name, "America." They were in the habit of saying *Anerica* and *šintas* (a hundred) instead of *šimtas;* likewise, instead of *dešimtas* (tenth) they said *dešintas,* most probably in accordance with the word *švintas* (holy) which was indeed a word very often on their lips.

This habit of pronouncing "n" instead of "m" gave them away at once to other eastern Highlanders. The latter liked to tease them by good-humoredly insisting that the people of

Puzionys were too lazy to close their mouths properly when they spoke.

In time, the explanations became more and more elaborate. It was said, for instance, that the villagers did not pronounce the letter "m" simply because the men were so fond of sucking on their pipes. A Puzionys man could spit or blow his nose or engage in a fist fight without once having to take out his pipe. Rumor had it that some of them actually refused to remove their pipes before taking a nap; and even the boys supposedly walked around with long pipes dangling from the left sides of their mouths like permanent fixtures. Small wonder, then, that the letter "m" was not a favorite among them, for it could not be pronounced correctly with pipe in mouth.

The following incident first brought fame to the village. There were two fine men known by the name of Gabrionys. The father was not yet old and the son not a great deal younger than his father. Both of them were very stubborn men.

One Wednesday, the father and the son, both at the same time, decided that they must go to the market. But each of them knew that the farm could not be left unattended. When the son jumped up and made ready to get the wagon out of the barn, his father seized him by the front of his shirt as if to hold him back. Turning around with a sudden movement, the son inadvertently knocked his father down and also fell down himself. They wrestled with each other on the ground and when they finally rose to their feet, their homemade jackets were rumpled and their caps had fallen off; only their pipes were intact, held as usual in the left side of their mouths, even though they had gone out completely.

"And now, quick, march to the village elder!" shouted the father. He felt humiliated and was very, very angry. "What will the world come to, when children begin to strike their parents?"

"Right! Let's go to the village elder!" agreed the son.

17

"We'll see what he has to say about parents who take their children for granted."

Both the men began to walk hurriedly across the village. But since the village elder lived at the very end of the village, the father and son felt, as they were walking, that they must stop for a smoke. They stopped and, facing each other, began to fill their pipes. When their pipes had been filled, they lit them with the same match for the sake of economy, even though they were still very cross with one another. But once they had puffed on their pipes for a while, they began to feel differently; their anger disappeared and they were no longer cross. Gabrionys, the son, kissed the hand of Gabrionys, the father, and both of them decided not to go to the market that day.

The story sounds like a legend. Believe it or not, just as you wish. It is characteristic of the people of Puzionys and it was probably made up by their neighbors to mock them a little. For the people of Puzionys were of an even and peaceful nature; they were cheerful and talkative and not in the least revengeful. It was this quality, not their pipes, which made their faces attractive.

The people of Puzionys knew how to tell a story about their neighbors as well, and it was quite an experience to listen to them. They took such pleasure in their embellishments and related the story with such enthusiasm and variation of tone that nobody could have accused them of laziness. For example, they would pronounce the word *tūkstantis* (a thousand) as *stūuukstančia,* with a long, drawn-out, whistling sound.

The people of Puzionys were indeed eastern Highlanders, yet they differed so much from the other Highlanders that they might have formed a distinct tribe on a separate island surrounded on all sides by water, marshes, or wide-stretching forestland. They were indeed different from the other eastern Highlanders, although there were no large stretches of water or forestland to set them apart. They did live, it is true, in a quiet, out-of-the-way place, even though

18

a tolerable highway cut across their fields. Their neighbors used it for traveling to church and to market.

The village of Puzionys was not visible from this highway. It stood on a much higher level, although not on top of a mountain (for there were no mountains to be found in the district) but at the summit of a steep slope that descended into a deep, wide valley. Since the village was out of the sight of travelers, they did not say much about it. Nobody cared or troubled much to inquire about the people who lived on this high plateau; no one asked whether they were people like themselves, moved by the same joys and sorrows and torn by the passions which could bring happiness or distress. The people of Puzionys lived just like other creatures of this world; like mice, for example, in their little caves, or like the pewits in the marshes in the valley down below, or even like other subjects of the Russian Empire. Nobody had said to them yet: "Wake up! Take a good look around you! It's high time you started a revolution! Can't you see that Russia, which has seized thousands of kilometers of land, neither knows how to make use of them nor allows the native people to bring any vitality into their lives?"

Such slogans were to resound in the ears of Puzionys somewhat later. In the meantime, the villagers led a life comparable to that of mice or other animals. It was a simple life, but even that simple life became complicated when passions overtook it; and, unlike the life of mice, it could provide themes for tragedies.

My tragedy concerns two young men and a woman. It struck the people of Puzionys quite unexpectedly and made their village notorious throughout the district.

THE TWO FRIENDS

THE FRIENDS, Jonas Butkys and Kazys Šnerva, did not differ much in appearance from the other men in Puzionys village. They were thin, of medium height and with ruddy complexions; they had attractive, well-formed noses, bright

19

blue eyes and cheerful expressions on their faces. They were both strong and sturdy peasants.

Jonas was the only son and heir of the Butkys family. His father had lived to see all the daughters marry, and when that anxiety was removed from his shoulders, he died in a Christian manner although he was not yet very old. The herbal medicine of his wife, Apolonija, which she had used to cure so many of her patients, was of no help to him at all. In the beginning, the widow was quite overcome by her grief and misfortune. But as time went on, she began to feel less downcast, especially when she saw that the farm, in spite of everything, remained standing in its place; and that her son, Jonas, who was a grown man now and a good man, too, was capable of managing it himself. He did not waste his time at the market for days on end, nor did he sit drinking at the tavern and listening to all manner of gossip. Jonas was too much of a man to waste his time in attending to women's tales. Nobody disturbed him and he did not disturb anyone. He was devoted to his farm with his whole heart and soul. There were no debts left when his father died and on the whole, life continued as of old. The less well-to-do villagers and the day laborers liked to work for the Butkys, which meant that Jonas was never short of help. Aunty herself was still a strong woman and did a great deal for her farm and family. She dressed her household like lords and ladies. It was indeed pleasant to live with such a family.

When her husband died, Apolonija transferred all her devotion to Jonas, her son, who was the new master of the farm. She loved him with the love of a mother for a child who had not done anything yet to upset her. Scarcely realizing it herself, she respected him as head of the household and left all the important decisions in his hands. However, she still continued to call him Joniukas, as of old. But on festive occasions or in serious times, which seemed to occur more and more often nowadays, she liked to refer to him as Jonas. Jonas liked to hear himself being addressed in this way; he felt as if he was being rewarded for a task which he had done especially well on the farm. Soon he grew important in his own eyes; but he recognized what a clever woman his mother was and how fortunate he was to have somebody like her to see him through the easy as well as the more difficult times.

Jonas began to doubt whether he would ever find a girl to equal his mother. He did not think it worth his while to look for a wife, for yet another mistress for his household. Even if he had found a sufficiently outstanding girl, which was most unlikely, where would he put his mother, who had done so much for him and for the family? In plain language, there was no room for two cats in one sack; they were bound to disagree with one another. And yet, to ask his mother to leave and to forego the profit which her many skills had brought to the farm was unthinkable.

Jonas was a man who idealized his mother completely and it seemed quite natural to him to think that he would remain a bachelor all his life. So he did not pay much attention to women when he was in town on Sundays and market days, or when he was at home in the village.

Kazys, who was his only good friend, loved and idealized Aunty in exactly the same way. He hardly knew himself why he loved and respected these two members of the Butkys family. Did he love Jonas because Aunty, his mother, was such a wonderful and exceptional woman, or did he love Aunty because she was his best friend's mother?

There were several members in the Šnerva family. Kazys' parents were still alive but they were elderly now and in poor health. All the daughters had been married off and only two brothers, besides Kazys, remained at home. All in all, there were still five people in the household. One would have thought that, with four men to till the land, a great deal could have been accomplished on the farm. But in reality, the family was quite poor. The sons were exceptionally good ploughmen; they worked hard and got on well together. None of them was a spendthrift; they were all decent and well-brought-up lads, and yet the farm did not flourish and money disappeared as if into a well.

It was clear to everyone that the parents were very poor managers; and they did not permit their children, as yet, to have any say in the running of the farm. Their mother, even when she was a young woman, was not a clever housewife. Now, she was old and far from strong. She spent most of her time curled up in the corner of her bed at the window, dozing or nodding; she had little energy for spinning or weaving or for taking care of the animals. She appeared to be more concerned with what went on in the street than in her kitchen, pantry or stables.

Her husband, too, was old and helpless. He was tall, thin and frail. When he buckled his narrow belt tightly, you could count his bones through his shirt. He rested, warmed himself, comforted himself and slept in his allotted place behind the stove. He sat up frequently in his bed, sighed deeply and cleared his throat. Then, slowly, he would let down his feet and climb down from the stove while he supported himself carefully with both hands, as if he were descending from a very high beam in the barn. He would put on his jacket and fasten the buckle of his belt, to all appearances as if he were getting ready to perform an unpleasant task ordered by the village elder. He said nothing to anyone. Sometimes he would go out through the door, but generally he would only stamp around on the floor and then unbuckle his belt, hang up his jacket and clamber up heavily onto his warm bed. There he would stay, moaning to himself as if he was extremely tired, like a man who had been hard at work in the barn, throwing the flax down, until his eyes began to close. He was like a cat suffering from old age.

Nobody showed the slightest interest in him or took care of him. One would have thought that at least his wife would have engaged him in conversation instead of spending her time looking through the window. But the old man did not have to ask for any favors from his children yet. He was still head of the household, after all, and he occupied the chief place at table, as well as ruling over the strings of his purse; it was kept in one of the pockets of his pants, which he never took off because he did not trust either his sons or the maid or the boy who came to help with the cattle. Not that there was much money in his purse.

His sons were used to poverty and did not complain about it to their parents at home or to friends in the village. They were healthy and pleasant-looking lads, and certainly they did not lack for food. Their pleasant disposition hid all that they may have been missing in this world.

The old people stayed at home while their children worked in the fields, and no disharmony was felt among them. There were no quarrels, no disagreements and no reproaches among them. The parents did not nag the children and the children did not despise the parents. Nevertheless, the household lacked joy. It was like a flock of hens without its rooster, or a beehive that had lost its queen-bee. There was an absence of womanly warmth which, as a rule, permeates a household.

Their mother, even when she was a young married woman, was sadly lacking in that quality, and her presence was scarcely felt in the house. One could have likened her to a piece of furniture or a wooden object in the room. So the house was not often visited by the neighbors, although nobody had a harsh word to say about the young Šnerva lads. The Šnervas kept themselves a little apart, and had it not been for the Butkys family, they would have lived out their lives almost as if in a monastery.

All the members of the Šnerva family awaited the visits of Jonas and his mother with the same kind of delight and eagerness one waits for a glimpse of the sun in the fall. On grey, dark days, which were often damp and dull as well, their arrival was like the arrival of the sun. At such times, the whole household came to life.

Aunty was the only person in the village who never forgot her neighbor, Mrs. Šnerva. After all, in the days

23

gone by, they had been godmothers to each other's children. They must have performed this mutual service at least three times. During the christening parties, they ate and drank at each other's houses and shared those happy hours of their lives. In time, when Mrs. Šnerva began to grow less strong, Aunty felt it her duty to visit her. After all, Aunty was the doctor and the pharmacist of the village.

Sometimes, they would happen to glance out of the window, and there would be Aunty coming out of her yard like a fox emerging from its lair. She would be carrying something underneath her apron. At such moments, Mrs. Šnerva would brighten up at once, supposing that her neighbor Apolonija was coming to visit them. Who can imagine their disappointment when they would see Aunty go past their house and hurry on along the street?

But on the happy occasions when Apolonija did come to visit, the entire household would come to life at once. Even the old man would show more vigor than usual, clearing his throat in a more contented manner and turning himself twice on his hard bed. The lads would smile from ear to ear and stand at attention, like soldiers, in the middle of the floor.

Apolonija would utter the customary greeting, "Blessed be Jesus Christ," and the whole household would respond with enthusiasm.

"Well, and how have you been keeping, dear?" she would say to Mrs. Šnerva. "I hope you're still taking my herbal medicine. I made it myself, you know. Drink it up and you'll get well quickly! Although, of course, we must not forget that it's God's will that we should all die eventually. After all, He, too, must miss his people, especially those who have been delayed here, down below."

"I drink it, I drink it. Thank you very much indeed. If it were not for your medicine, I hate to think where I would be now."

They would whisper to each other for hours on end, these two old neighbors. Both would talk at the same time

24

with their heads close together, each scarcely listening to what the other was saying, but well pleased that they had this opportunity to tell one another all that burdened their hearts and minds. First, they would talk about their ailments, and then about their housekeeping worries; and, if there was still time left, they would begin to indulge in reminiscences.

On such occasions, Mrs. Šnerva became a different person. It was amazing that there was still so much life left in her. She had such a strong desire to live and to see people, even though she was as good as confined to her bed. She bore little resemblance to the mummy-like figure that had been sitting in front of the window just a while ago.

The young lads, in the meantime, remained standing in the middle of the room as if attending a service at the Orthodox church. They listened eagerly to the women's conversation without attempting to take part in it or to interrupt them. They were pleased that their mother was happy and were grateful in their hearts to Aunty for making, at least from time to time, the patient's life more endurable. Only when the guest was taking her leave did they begin to speak, all of them at once, and still talking, they would escort her to the gates of her yard. Then they would wait again for her next visit, as if for some epoch-making adventure, and would eagerly count the hours and the days in great expectancy.

Jonas came to call on them also, to see his friend Kazys, but he caused no great change in their life. All the same, even the visits of Jonas Butkys were something to look forward to in their uneventful lives.

Kazys was the only member of the Šnerva family to visit the Butkyses. He visited them very often; whenever he had a free minute, he would go over to see them. He liked to put in an appearance at their house before setting out on a journey or attempting any new task. He could never forget his childhood when he had been as sure of his place on Aunty's lap as Jonas himself was. Now he was too old for that, but he would have felt happy had he been able to rest his head on her lap, if just for a moment.

Lately, however, Kazys had grown to be embarrassed by Aunty's hospitality. He felt that he was accepting too much from her. Aunty, for her part, considered it her duty to offer some sort of refreshment to her callers. She rejoiced with her whole heart to see her visitors. It made no difference whether they were male or female, old or young. She always had a good word for everyone. And whether they wanted it or not, she would offer them things to eat, either a piece of cheese or perhaps a pancake; she put these things straight into their hands if they refused to sit down at table. But if there was neither cheese nor a pancake to be had, she grew desperate and would wave her arms about, saying:

"My dear man (or woman or child, whichever it might be), I can't let you go without giving you at least something to drink."

She would reach out at once for a tin cup and fill it with sweet beer or fruit juice; and who could refuse her? She never took "no" for an answer. Why, she would even catch up with you in the passage if you tried to escape.

To the village people, it was no hardship to have something extra to eat or drink, and most visitors would simply kiss Aunty's hand in gratitude for the refreshment as well as for the goodness of her heart. They did not stand on ceremony.

Kazys could not rightly complain of hunger, because since growing to manhood he hardly ever felt that he had had enough to eat on rising from the table. But to offer food to a hungry person was to offend his pride. Therefore, Kazys tried to avoid visiting his neighbors whenever he thought that they might be getting ready to eat. But even though Kazys found it embarrassing to accept offerings of food these days, he could hardly ever bring himself to say no to Aunty.

✧   ✧   ✧

The following are two episodes from the day-to-day lives of these two neighboring families.

Kazys knocked on the door of the Butkys house boldly, felt blindly for the latch, opened the door and walked inside.

"Good morning, Aunty dear! Where is Jonas this morning?"

"Good morning to you, Kazys!" replied Aunty without troubling to turn around from the stove where she was busily preparing breakfast. "What do you want him for so early in the day? Wait for him, then; he'll be back from the stables any time now. It looks as if the mare has cast her foal. Jonas is as pleased about it as I am on my midwifery visits. Wait for him a minute and then we'll all have breakfast together and you can talk to him to your heart's content."

"Thank you very much, Aunty. But I won't have breakfast with you this time. My people are sitting down to it at home and I'm in rather a hurry. Won't Jonas come and have breakfast with me, this time? You see, the Russians are here to talk about draining the land, and they're waiting for an answer." Kazys tried to excuse himself this way.

"Some new project underfoot again, heaven forbid! It doesn't do to ask for too much in this life. New inventions only harm people. No good ever comes of them. I can tell you that much, my lad! Look at our girls nowadays! How they brush their hair up and cover their foreheads with fringes! And as for the men, attaching red and blue hoods to the collars of their coats; whoever saw the like! And the new styles of the women's coats. To say nothing of the new gigs that they're making. Such fashions are surely for the gentry and not for us ordinary folk. Please stay, Kazys; you can talk things over with Jonas at breakfast."

Kazys stayed. What else could he do? He liked being here among the Butkys family, for here he found the womanly warmth that was sadly lacking at home. Whenever, in the course of the day, he was upset or felt depressed, he longed to run in to Aunty. She could tell at a glance what

27

was wrong with him. And after he had exchanged a few words with her, he felt himself to be a different person.

Soon Jonas came running into the house.

"Mother! Kazys! There has never ever been such a beautiful foal in the whole village. Come over and see! No, I'm not sorry now that I took the trouble to lead the mare over to the estate. . . ."

All three of them hurried to the stables. They came back into the room after a while, very much impressed by the mare's offspring.

"She is black as tar," said Aunty. "A dark bay would have been more attractive, more in keeping with the rest of our horses. They say that witches like to ride on black horses. Besides, black surely reminds you of the devil. But perhaps I'm being silly. Perhaps all such superstition is nonsense. May God bless the creature!"

"Its left hind foot is white, Mother! And there is a star on its forehead. Don't you worry, it'll shine like a lamp in the dark to dispel all evil spirits," said Jonas.

"Some foal, I call it! Why, it's as big as a three-month-old colt," put in Kazys, and he blew his nose with feeling.

While they were discussing the new arrival in such an enthusiastic manner, before they realized it, they found themselves seated at the table, where a steamy dish of flat cakes covered with sauce awaited them.

"Help yourselves to breakfast, children." Aunty interrupted their rejoicing. "Do eat while the sauce is still hot."

But Kazys caught himself in time and said, "Really, Aunty, here I am again. I always seem to be sitting down at your table. I ought to be eating at home."

It was true that just about this time Kazys' family was gathering for breakfast. One could even see the men, in their shirtsleeves, sitting at the table by the window. Kazys would have had a breakfast just as good as this in his own house.

"It's quite all right, Kazys. It doesn't make much difference whether you eat here or at home. You are not a stranger, after all. So eat as much as you can. Remember, our Jonas sits down at your table often enough." Aunty chatted on as if to herself, especially since the men were fully occupied with eating and had no time to listen to her.

"Oh, Jonas! Your new foal made me quite forget for a moment the reason why I've come to see you," Kazys exclaimed when he had finished eating and had wiped his fingers. "Come over to our house, now. The Russians are waiting there. They have an idea that we should drain our fields by digging a canal a verst long."

"And where will the water go to?" inquired Jonas.

"The water? Why, down into the valley, into the Pewit Valley."

"Yes, but it will ruin the highway. And a bridge will have to be built, of course. No doubt, we shall be responsible for repairing it. And that would be no joke, as you know, with all the building materials being brought from the forests, fifteen miles away frome home! Do what you like, but I myself am not for it. Let the meadows stay as they are. In hot weather, they dry off without the help of a canal."

"That's exactly what I think. And the whole village, too, you may be sure. Well, let's go and tell them, then. I didn't want to take the responsibility of speaking for the whole village myself."

The two young men rose as quickly from the table as they had sat down. When Kazys was already on his way out of the room, he seized one of Aunty's hands, in which she was holding an oven peel, and hurriedly bent down to kiss it. But instead of kissing her hand, his kiss landed on the handle of the oven peel. Aunty smiled affectionately as she saw the two men through the door.

It was true that their decision reflected the view of the whole village. In the eyes of the people of Puzionys, the idea of digging a deep canal, a verst long, seemed as great an undertaking as building a railroad to the moon. After all, they had not even troubled to dig ditches in the streets of their village to drain the water off; and in the fall, as well as at other times, they suffered for it.

On higher ground, they had fields of good quality. Had they been drained, these fields would have been twice as good. The peasants of Puzionys would certainly have been well-to-do farmers then. As it was, even now they felt that they could afford to neglect their poorer meadows in the valley, which were quite large and a whole kilometer away from the village.

THE MATCHMAKERS

KAZYS AND JONAS were not in the habit of frequenting village dances. What would they have done there, since they did not know how to dance? They were not much interested in girls. At least, nobody had ever noticed them paying any attention to girls in general or showing a liking for any particular girl. But Jonas and Kazys liked to spend some of their evenings together with the other young people of the village. Usually, on such evenings, the girls would sing as they busied themselves with their spinning wheels, and the young men would stand around the table plaiting rope and chatting among themselves. Although the girls formed a separate circle, they and the boys took a great delight in one another's company. When the evening was over, they would go home satisfied with themselves and with the work which they had accomplished.

Kazys and Jonas were the most sought-after lads of the Puzionys village. Many covert glances were directed towards them, and they could not help feeling very pleased. When they used to walk home at the end of such evenings, one of the girls sometimes managed to catch up with them and made advances towards them, saying: "Good evening, dear inseparable twins! Haven't you broken up yet, or are you still two beans in one pod?" But more often than not, she would receive an abrupt and even harsh reply.

Such offhand treatment offended the girls. How were

they to know whether Jonas and Kazys were unmannerly by nature or whether they merely pretended to be? The girls began to leave them alone. If they wanted to be treated like strangers, let them be strangers then!

The only woman whom Jonas and Kazys idealized was Aunty, or Apolonija Butkys. They had not found anyone yet who could take her place or even stand up to compare with her.

March was usually a cold and difficult month to get through for the old people. Mrs. Šnerva gave up her customary post at the windowsill and took to lying down in her bed. One morning, when the house was quite empty, Kazys came into the room as soon as he had finished chopping wood. His mother called to him in a weak voice.

"Kazimieras, come closer to me and listen to what I have to say. I am growing weaker day by day. I've not been much of a housekeeper to you, I know, although you haven't reproached me for it or said one word about it. I know that you love me, your mother, and I am grateful to you. God will repay you for your patience with me."

As Kazys listened to her serious words, he felt very humble and for the first time, without experiencing a sense of duty, he sat down quickly on the edge of his mother's bed and looked with affection into her old and wrinkled face.

His mother was not beautiful any more. Her face was wrinkled and her nose seemed to have lost its shape. All the same, as Kazys looked at her, he felt that he had never loved her so much before. A gentle and sorrowful force seized his heart as he realized that his mother was preparing herself to leave this world. His eyes filled with tears. He bent down quickly, seized his mother's hand which lay limp on the blanket, and kissed it with feeling.

The old woman stroked his head. "You're a good child, Kazys. May the good Lord grant you happiness. You must look for a wife, now. For a young and able girl to help you with the farm."

31

"I wish you wouldn't talk about it, Mother! We want you to stay in your place. You're certainly not in anybody's way! I'm still young. There'll be time enough to think of getting married later on."

They went on talking for a long time, the two of them, as if attempting to make up for the silence of so many years. They spoke of the farm, of friends and enemies; they mentioned the church and God but said not a word more about marrying.

Nevertheless, his mother's advice and her anxiety that he should look around for a wife had made a great impression on Kazys, and in his heart he began to think seriously about it.

In his own village, there was no girl whom he liked or who could have stood up to comparison with his beloved Aunty. But one feast day, when he was attending Mass in the neighboring town and was standing solemnly facing the altar as he waited for the priest to appear, a clatter of heels interrupted his pious mood. He had taken a place in the middle of the church, close to the central aisle. Kazys turned his head imperceptibly and saw a very lovely girl hurrying into the church with small but energetic and firm steps. Admittedly, her beauty consisted merely of a full, girlish face and a healthy complexion which had grown even more highly colored because of her lateness. Her hair was fair, like that of the angels painted on the walls and ceiling of the church. It was secured with blue ribbons.

Not that her looks mattered all that much to Kazys. His aesthetic standards were not high. But there was something about her face, her shoulders, her height and the way she held herself that reminded him of Aunty. Like Aunty, she was small and plump with a tranquil, kindly expression in her eyes. Her whole bearing in church differed considerably from that of the other country girls; it pleased him. He saw other country women genuflect before the altar in a clumsy, graceless manner; they fell down in front of it like sacks of flour, he thought, but not so this girl. It occurred

32

to Kazys suddenly to wonder, was this the girl intended for him as his future wife?

Although like most of the villagers, Kazys was a pious young man, from the moment he saw the girl he was lost to the world and unaware what went on around him. When, at long last, Mass ended and the congregation began to leave the church, he was surprised to find himself close to her, and he tried to protect her from the crowds of people pressing towards the door.

When he was in the church yard, he noticed a young man whom he knew standing close to the gates and filling his pipe. The young man called to the girl in greeting: "Hello, Anelja! What has brought you here, today? It must be quite a distance for you to come from your village."

"I've brought my wool to be dyed. We haven't such facilities in our town, you know."

Kazys, feeling in an especially good mood, shook hands with his friend and was about to join them in their conversation when the girl nodded her head briefly to them and walked away.

"Oh, who is she?" inquired Kazys as he yawned and tried to appear indifferent.

His friend saw through him at once. "So you've noticed her, too, haven't you? No wonder. She's the most attractive girl in the whole of the next parish. She's a farmer's daughter. Beautiful, as you can see, but there's no money to be had in her dowry. The matchmakers have not neglected her, I can assure you. But she's undecided still. Anelja hasn't much time to waste, though. She must be close to twenty-four. I'll be your matchmaker, if you like. But she lives a long way from here and a long way from your village, too!"

"All right," said Kazys without wavering. "Don't let's waste any time."

"I'll go and look for her, then, and tell her to expect us next Sunday after Mass."

They parted, and Kazys could think of nothing but this lovely girl who appeared to be so serious; she did not blush

33

when strangers greeted her, even though they seemingly could not take their eyes from her. She must be like Aunty. She must have seen something of the world, he thought to himself.

And Kazys began to picture a future life shared with this girl. A gay life it would be, full of joy and happiness; but, as he hastened to add in his thoughts, it would not exclude his friends, the Butkyses. He was so carried away by his imagination that his ears and neck grew red. Kazys was not used to such strong emotions and the wild rush of blood into his head made him feel dizzy and faint.

"It will all come true, please God." Kazys repeated the same phrase over and over again, scarcely knowing himself what he was saying. Suddenly, he was filled with longing for the girl.

As soon as he had reached home, he unharnessed his horse and, forgetting all about the dinner which was waiting for him, hurried over to the Butkys house.

"Aunty, Aunty, you'll never guess what has happened! I've found my own!" he shouted with enthusiasm from the threshold.

Apolonija was taken aback. "What are you talking about, Kazys? What've you found? Your own sheep, your own pig?" She looked at Kazys blankly.

"A girl, that's what I've found." For the first time in many years, he embraced Aunty and kissed her on the lips.

Now Apolonija understood what was the matter with him. But she did not show any gladness, as one might have expected. On the contrary, she was so taken aback by the announcement that she crossed herself. It was a good minute before she recovered.

"Such news you've brought me! Now you'll think of nothing else, all the time. Don't you go and make a fool of yourself! You don't even know the girl. Perhaps she belongs to somebody else already. Where's she from? Where was she born and who are her parents?"

Aunty's questions and doubts hit Kazys like a bucketful

34

of cold water. All his former boyishness and enthusiasm left him. He realized how childish he had been.

"How can I tell you, Aunty? I don't know much about her. I've seen her today for the first time. She lives a long way from here."

Apolonija clapped her hands on hearing such an explanation. "From another parish, did you say? From a different part of the country? You must be out of your mind, Kazys! Why, before a man puts a wheel to an axle, he measures it; because if the wheel's too low, the whole wagon will go lopsided; and if the wheel is too high, why that's even worse. But to choose a wife just like that! A person who will be responsible for your happiness for the rest of your life! And what will happen later on, if she's not the right one for you?"

Kazys collapsed on the bench, feeling that there was no strength left in him. With his sleeve, he began to wipe drops of perspiration from his forehead. "She is a very devout girl . . . and clever, too. The whole neighborhood is loud in her praise. She's beautiful, Aunty, as well," Kazys continued in a scarcely audible voice.

"That's all very well, my child. Often, we cannot help but feel we like or dislike someone; but you must wait and pray, Kazys, before making such an important decision. Perhaps it would be better for you to marry a girl from your own village, even if she's not so clever or good-looking. At least, you'd know what to expect of her."

Jonas, who had come into the room, stood listening to their conversation with a smile. He felt as though he had been already invited to be best man. "Well, Kazys, my happy bridegroom, when are you going to ask for her hand? Can't I be of help? I'll be your matchmaker, if you like. I don't know any of the appropriate speeches, and I don't like boasting and lying to people, but I would certainly like to see your girl. Oh, we won't bother about the speeches, in any case. I'll simply tell her family that you're my best friend, which means that they could not possibly find a better

35

fellow than you." Jonas chattered on gaily like someone
who was really looking forward to a wedding. His mother
was not surprised.

"I don't need a matchmaker, thank you. I have one already. But you're welcome to come with me, if you like."

They began to look forward to the following Sunday
with great eagerness. Jonas thought of nothing else but how
to marry his friend off as quickly as possible. The prospect
of having a new person living nearby, to whom their stories
and jokes had not been told, filled him with delight.

But Kazys was overcome with alarm, like a man about
to be nailed to a cross. As the days passed, he felt no happiness. On the contrary, he could not sleep and he could
not eat; he even lost weight. His eyes shone feverishly, his
cheeks fell in and there were black rings under his eyes.
He looked like a person recovering from an illness or like
someone who had been drinking heavily. At last, he felt as
if he could no longer contain himself and on Saturday
evening he strode angrily over to the Butkys house.

"I'm not going tomorrow, Jonas, I'd like you to know,"
he exclaimed in a troubled voice. "I'm not ready yet for
marriage. I've been feeling so uneasy lately; I've all but
hanged myself from a nail."

Apolonija and Jonas were very much surprised by what
they heard. Jonas was so disappointed by this announcement
that he lost his temper there and then. He had gone to some
trouble; he had made all the necessary preparations and
therefore the journey could not be put off now.

Even Apolonija, for once, was of the same opinion as
Jonas. It was surely wrong and cowardly to change one's
mind at the last moment!

"You must go, Kazys. All is in God's hands. Who knows,
perhaps everything will turn out for the best. You need a
wife, too, what with your ailing mother and everything."
Aunty went on talking to him at great length as if trying to
persuade herself that what she said was true, whereas in her
heart of hearts she felt that nothing good would come of it.

Early the following morning, Jonas and Kazys set off to collect the matchmaker. They felt nervous and uneasy. While Jonas busied himself with the horse, whipping and scolding the animal, Kazys sat in the gig passively like a sheep on its way to the slaughterhouse. He addressed not a word to Jonas, but sat with his shoulders bent forward and his eyes focused on his leg, which he had thrown over the side of the gig as if there were not room enough for it elsewhere.

Jonas glanced at Kazys several times. He could not help feeling annoyed by his strange posture and downcast looks. "Don't you know how to sit up straight, man? Why, you look like a horse on his last legs."

But when they called on the matchmaker, he declined to go along with them. "Since there are two of you already, you can do without me. As it happens, I'm busy today and can't easily spare the time." He gave them directions how to reach the village, described the route that they were to follow and advised them not to waste time but to begin their journey straight after Mass.

Kazys found himself in the same church where he had first seen Anelja, and he chose to stand in exactly the same place as before. He began to listen eagerly for the clatter of her heels. He forgot completely that this was not Anelja's parish and that she seldom came to pray in this church.

When Mass was over, the two friends purchased a bottle of wine and a bottle of whiskey and made ready to go. But all at once, for no apparent reason, Jonas was overcome with shyness; he felt his cheeks blush at the very thought of having to stand in as matchmaker for his childhood friend. He began to regret, from the depth of his heart, his casual offer of help.

"You know, Kazys, you'll just have to go on alone and be your own matchmaker. The devil take your girls! No, I haven't it in me to visit these people."

"But it's too late now, Jonas. We've paid for the wine

37

and the whiskey. Besides, I can't very well go without a matchmaker, and Anelja's parents are expecting us."

They did not hurry overmuch on their journey. They wanted Anelja's people to have time to set the house straight and prepare a meal on coming home from church. But they reached the village soon enough.

It was just like any other village. They drove into the farmyard, which was neatly swept and put to order as on the eve of a feast day. One could see at a glance that guests were expected and very special guests, too.

Anelja's father came out to meet them himself. He was a handsome, fair-haired man of just over forty. His wife followed him out of the house. She was a good-looking woman of about the same age. They were pleasant, likeable people who did not give themselves airs.

"Ah, and where is the matchmaker? I can only see two bridegrooms," Mr. Kepelė said jokingly, as if to himself, for he was not more than ten years older than his future son-in-law. "Are you the young people we have been expecting?"

"We are, indeed. The matchmaker couldn't come, after all. I'm Jonas Butkys. And here is my friend, Kazimieras Šnerva. We're both from Puzionys. I am taking the matchmaker's place, you see. But I'm a new hand at it and not much good at praising people."

Mr. Kepelė laughed good naturedly and said that, to put matters briefly, Anelja was their only child and that they were not in the least ashamed of her, either; but if it was money the young men were after, then they had come in vain.

"No, no," Jonas put in quickly. "We're not interested in money. We are interested in the bride and we've heard what a beautiful girl your daughter is."

They went indoors. The table was laid and the room was neat and tidy. Everything was in its place. Anelja greeted them in a kind manner and spoke to them as though they were old friends.

"Well, Anelja, which of these two young men is the bridegroom and which is the matchmaker? Come and guess," her

38

father said to her. Anelja looked at Jonas and Jonas looked at Anelja.

Jonas started to blush, as if he had done something wrong, and followed the girl with his eyes. He felt happy to be here among them, happier than he had ever been before in his life.

The unusual similarity among all three members of the Kepelė family impressed Kazys most of all. Each one of them appeared to be pleased with life, contented and in good health.

"Like three full ears of wheat," he thought to himself. "No, no, they were much more like three beautiful red apples." And he stared at the family with delight, forgetting all his former uneasiness. Jonas, his matchmaker, was left to do all the talking.

After lunch, Mr. Kepelė invited his guests to inspect the farm. Then Jonas was called upon to entertain Anelja while Kazys talked to her parents. Jonas was in high spirits and spoke with enthusiasm about his new black foal, which had a beautiful white star on its forehead.

Anelja, for her part, listened to Jonas' every word attentively. She had never met such a talkative and lively young man before. She had never liked anyone as much as she liked Jonas. Although they had been talking to each other for no more than an hour or so, Anelja felt as if she had known Jonas all her life. They seemed to have so much in common.

Eventually, even Kazys began to notice that his "matchmaker" was enjoying remarkable success with his intended. To his surprise, he grew jealous and, breaking off his conversation with Anelja's parents abruptly, he walked up to the pair and said to Jonas in a dry voice, "Surely you, Jonas, ought to be talking to Anelja's parents, and I to Anelja. We seem to have our roles mixed up." And without further ceremony, he pushed Jonas away in the direction of the older people.

As soon as Anelja's mother had shown Kazys the storehouse and Anelja's dowry chest, which was full of excellent linens, Kazys led Anelja aside. He put his arm lightly across her plump shoulders and, holding her by the elbows, said to her, "I like you very much, Anelja, as I've never liked anyone before in all my life except for Jonas' mother, Aunty, of course. But that's a different story altogether. Aunty is sixty years old and more. Don't you think that we have been meant for each other? I would be so happy if you were to marry me."

Anelja had never been spoken to in such a way before. She blushed violently and felt hot and cold at once. But looking straight into Kazys' eyes, she said, "As you know, I'm twenty-four years old. I do not wish to be an old maid. It's a wonder that we have met at all, when you think how far away Puzionys is from my village. I'll think about it. I won't say no."

"Have you heard, dear parents-in-law? Anelja is not throwing me out," exclaimed Kazys gaily.

"Nor are we, nor are we," replied Anelja's mother, sad as she was at the idea of losing her only daughter to a stranger who lived so far away from them. Mother and daughter fell into each other's arms weeping and the men blew their noses hard. It was time for Kazys and Jonas to go.

Anelja's parents saw their guests off through the gate and remained for a long time in the yard, talking.

"Such fine young men!" exclaimed Mr. Kepelė.

"You're quite right, you know. They are the pleasantest young people I've ever met. They were certainly more interested in Anelja than in her dowry," Anelja's mother added as an afterthought.

"May the Almighty bless them!"

"Well, and what have you got to say, Anelja?" Mr. Kepelė asked, turning to his daughter.

"Let me see. How shall I put it, Father? I liked both of them. Both Jonas and Kazys seem like such pleasant young men. If anything, perhaps I liked the matchmaker better. Still, I'm ready to marry the one who has asked for my hand."

KAZYS AND JONAS

THE TWO YOUNG matchmakers drove out of Mr. Kepelė's yard in style. As they drove past the cross which stood near the farm buildings, Jonas raised his hat briefly. But as soon as they entered the main road, he urged the horse on to a full trot. There was little to attend to now, and soon the two young men were lost in their thoughts.

Kazimieras could think of nothing but Anelja. He recalled the scene that had taken place in the storehouse and regretted that he had had so little opportunity to show his affection for the girl. If only he dared to jump out of the gig now, on the pretense that he had left something behind at the farm, he could see Anelja again and perhaps even embrace her and kiss her. But he merely glanced over his shoulder once or twice at the receding village and continued to sit in the gig with his left foot dangling over the side. Soon, he was lost in daydreaming as he imagined the years to come when Anelja would be installed as mistress of his household. She would be with him then, and not miles away as she was now.

Jonas, for his part, felt a bitter taste in his mouth, as if he was suffering from heartburn. He kept recalling his meeting with Anelja and what had taken place between them a little while before. What a fool he had been! Never, for a moment, had he imagined that such women as Anelja existed. Nor had he known how good it was to talk to someone as young and sympathetic as this girl.

To make matters worse, Kazimieras' success with Anelja made Jonas feel uncomfortable. All his life, as far back as he could remember, Jonas was used to being the most important young man in his village. Suddenly, through no fault of his own, he saw himself left behind and neglected. He had tried to live a good and decent life, and was this the reward? As far as he could see, the prize of life had gone to his second-in-command. What a prize, too! He felt the injustice of it all so strongly that he could scarcely bear to look at Kazys.

41

Jonas was feeling very jealous. He wanted to talk to Kazys and reproach him for having won the best prize in the lottery quite undeservedly. But he said nothing. He wanted to quarrel and fight with Kazys; he wanted to leave him, to jump out of the cart and finish his journey on foot. But he remained where he was, and they finished their journey in silence.

"Thanks for the ride," was all that Kazys said after they had reached home; and, without so much as a glance in Jonas' direction, he started for his own yard.

"Don't mention it," replied Jonas dryly.

All at once, it occurred to Jonas that it was only due to his mother's position in the village that he had been made much of all his life. By himself, he supposed, he counted for nothing. Moreover, he foresaw that, in time, as his mother grew to be really old, people would not come to visit them any more. On the other hand, Kazys' household would increase in popularity every day.

Jonas grew sad and melancholy at the thought. He felt as if he were being led to his grave alive. But he knew that he must not think such thoughts. Surely it was wrong to think in this way. Perhaps God Himself was rewarding Kazimieras for his goodness by giving him such a wife as Anelja. Was it not Providence that caused them to meet in the first place? If only Jonas didn't like Anelja so much. Ah, what a girl she was! With a wife like that, Kazys wouldn't have the time or the inclination to visit Jonas any more.

Yet Jonas' heart said to him, "Don't talk such nonsense! Kazys won't stay glued forever to his wife. They won't forbid you to come and visit them. It will be just as it was in the past, when both our families were happy."

Apolonija was surprised to notice that Jonas was taking such a long time to unharness the horse and put the gig away. Usually, he would come into the house as soon as he arrived. He was always so eager to share his experiences with her, to tell her all that he had seen.

When, at long last, Jonas came into the house, he said

42

nothing. He sat down on a bench without even remembering to take his cap off. Was he ill? Or had he lost something? Was something the matter with his horse?

"Jonas, what is wrong with you? Wasn't your journey a success? You look so unlike yourself," his mother said.

"Oh, Kazys is very lucky. His bride-to-be is a beautiful and lovely girl. You must have been just like her, Mother, when you were a young girl. Now you'll see—Anelja will draw all the hearts in the village and all the eyes, too. She and Kazimieras will be the first family in the village instead of us."

"You're not jealous of them, are you, Jonas? God forbid! We're not going to compete with one another. What we have, we have; nobody is going to take it away from us."

Nevertheless, Apolonija herself began to feel a little envious of the young bride-to-be. She grew conscious, too, for the first time in her life, of the never ending competition between parents and children. The children are the winners as a rule, simply because they live longer. Her jealousy was of the kind often felt so harshly in the relationship between a mother-in-law and a daughter-in-law.

Apolonija was not pleased at the prospect of Kazimieras' wedding. The idea that her beloved Kazys was soon to be the husband of such a worthy person did not make her in the least happy. She could not even bring herself to pronounce Anelja's name, and referred to the young woman simply as "she" whenever the subject came up.

✱　　✱　　✱

The banns were posted and the three week waiting period was soon over. During that time, Kazys went to see Anelja as often as he could. He was happy, and for the first time in his life, he did not wish to share his happiness with his Aunty.

Apolonija understood. In any case, she did not have time to waste because most of the wedding preparations had been left up to her. She seemed to put her whole heart into the

43

affair, too: one would have thought that it was Jonas and not Kazys who was getting married. But, to tell the truth, she felt as though she was getting ready for the funeral of some dearly-loved friend.

Jonas made many trips to the mill. He brought home a good supply of wheat, barley and rye flour. Cakes were baked, geese were roasted, hams were prepared and the cheeses made—yellow and soft as wax they were, as only Apolonija knew how to make them. Food was made to last not for one day but for a good number of days. After all, many people had been invited and not just from their own village.

Such a wedding it was, too! The young village people themselves arranged for the illumination of the yard; they hollowed out red and white beetroots and put burning candles inside. There were three musicians, to say nothing of a man from the town who, from time to time, would lend a hand in playing a barrel organ. There were wreaths hung everywhere, and for two whole days everybody, including the shepherd boys, had a wonderful time and were given so much to eat and drink that nobody in the whole village could remember a wedding like it!

The bride was beautiful to look at. She was a woman at the height of her maturity, not a mere slip of a girl. She was serious, but had such a lovely, feminine smile that the young lads vied quite openly for her attention. The smiles and the image of this charming young bride were to haunt them for a long time afterwards.

There were gifts for many of the wedding guests: a scarf for one, a sash or tablecloth for another. And the presents made them think even more highly—if such a thing were possible—of the new Mrs. Šnerva. She was the subject of every conversation.

Jonas, as the best man and most important guest at the wedding, made the most of his privileges and enjoyed himself as he had never done before in his life. Although he danced with all the girls, he also seized every available op-

44

portunity to dance with Anelja, and would whirl her round and round the floor until Kazys reappeared on the scene. Jonas knew how to speak and to laugh and dance with a girl in an open, friendly manner. He was the envy of all the other young men at the wedding.

When at last the celebration was over, the bride's parents, who had stayed with their daughter until the end, made ready to go home. As they drove out of the Šnerva yard, both of them began to speak at once.

"Have we done the right thing, d'you suppose, to hand her over like this to her new mother-in-law and father-in-law?" Anelja's father asked.

"Don't you worry," her mother replied. "They'll come over to see us in a week's time. Our Anelja won't have a bad life, you know."

"Perhaps you're right," the bride's father said then. "Kazimieras seems to love her with his whole heart. And his brother is quiet and sensible. Let's hope that the one who is in the army is just as pleasant. The parents are old and feeble; they won't live long. Anelja's mother-in-law won't be a burden to her. Why, she hasn't even the strength to scold her from her bed!"

"But it's such a distance from us, all the same," Anelja's mother went on. "I'm beginning to miss our daughter already. I've had her under my wing for so many years." With that, she began to weep softly into her handkerchief.

"Well, what can you expect? It will be very strange and dull without her, to say the least. If the other son, the one who is away in the army now, would come home and get married, Anelja and Kazys could come and live with us. We could buy more land . . . and be together again."

Mrs. Kepelė listened to her husband attentively. She approved wholeheartedly of what he said. It was as if her husband had given voice to her own thoughts. Little by little, both of them began to feel better.

The days that followed the wedding festivities were wonderful and gay ones for the Šnervas. It was clear to everyone

45

that Kazimieras was very happy and did not try to hide his feelings. He was so proud of himself for having built a family nest.

Anelja's parents-in-law, as we have said, were old and ailing. Kazimieras' father had refused to leave his bed throughout the whole noisy upheaval of the wedding. His mother, on the other hand, seemed to welcome the presence of the new bride. And Anelja, for her part, did what she could to make her mother-in-law more comfortable. She gave the old woman her own new, thick blanket which was padded with cotton wool and was the first of its kind to be seen at Puzionys.

"Thank you, child, for taking care of me so well in my illness and old age. May God grant you a peaceful and painless old age, when your time comes. What a good, warm blanket it is. Bless you!"

Anelja was pleased with the way she treated the ailing woman and Kazimieras, with the latter's blessing, thanked her in his own fashion. He took both her hands in his, looked deeply into her eyes and kissed her without a word. Kazimieras was very devoted to his parents, but he did not know how to show his feelings. Therefore, expressions of affection and gentleness coming from the woman he loved were especially dear to him.

When three weeks had passed, Kazimieras' mother began to feel quite ill and requested the priest to be called. She wanted to give the young couple her blessing, and asked them to live in peace and to love each other always.

"I think, Kazimieras, that you're happily married. God has given you a good wife. Be good to her."

Kazimieras began to cry. He was moved, perhaps not so much by the old woman's preparation for death as by her praise of Anelja. But he dried his tears, harnessed the horse and, without a word, set off to bring the priest.

Mrs. Šnerva died and was buried shortly thereafter; and her husband followed her to the grave in the very same week. The neighbors were astonished at two deaths so close to each other in one family, but they all knew what a good son Kazimieras had been and they began to look upon the passing away of his parents as a blessing. It made room for the young ones, they said.

But this was not what Kazys thought. To him, his parents, although admittedly old and ailing, had always been the true blessing of the household. He was extremely sorrowful and not himself all that week, and was lavish with money for the funerals. After all, hadn't he received a full hundred rubles as part of Anelja's dowry from Mr. Kepelė, his father-in-law?

The illness and death of his parents, so soon after the wedding, gave Kazys little opportunity to get to know his wife better. But as soon as life returned to its normal course, he tried to open his heart to Anelja. With both of his parents gone at once, there was a dreadful emptiness in his life.

"You know what, Anelja, I can't remember the time when mother didn't take part in organizing things on the farm. Even though, for a long time, she wasn't well and sat there on her bed with her feet tucked under her, she was always there in the house when one wanted to speak to her. And now the bed is empty. Every time I go into her room, it's as if a knife went through my heart."

Kazimieras longed for Anelja to console and comfort him. Suddenly, he wanted to tell her of everything that had happened to him in the past and, with her help, to replace his old life with a new one. But Anelja seemed to pay little attention to him. She busied herself with her household tasks and replied to all that Kazimieras was trying to tell her in an unwilling and absent-minded fashion.

Kazimieras felt let down and disappointed in his wife. Who would make the sun shine in the dark days, now? Where was he to look for shelter against the storms of life? His parents had never been indifferent to him, as old and sick as they were. In the past, whenever he was upset or worried about anything, they would listen to him and give

47

him all the moral support that they could. Neither of them had ever answered him with a cold, "Yes . . . ?" as Anelja was doing now. As far as Kazys was concerned, it was the start of their unhappiness, an unhappiness that opened up suddenly before them.

At times, Kazimieras felt that he would have liked to tease Anelja a little. Whistling and singing under his breath, he would enter the house when Anelja was occupied with her household tasks. How he would have liked to embrace her, to twirl her around and around in the middle of the floor, and to kiss her. But it was clear that Anelja did not share his mood. She lived with him dutifully, as a wife is expected to live with her husband. She did not avoid her responsibilities, but that was all. At first, when Kazys was head over heels in love with her, he did not even notice her apparent coolness. But as time went on, he could not help but notice Anelja's lack of love for him.

Kazimieras felt disillusioned and disappointed in his marriage. Married love had not come anywhere near his expectations. Why? he wondered. His heart told him that when love was added to love, more love resulted. Then married love should have been much sweeter. But when only one side could contribute its share of love. . . .

As the days passed, Kazimieras began to see how passive Anelja was towards him. All his happiness and high spirits evaporated and he no longer went gaily about his tasks. He began to see his wife in a new light and with a new understanding.

But Anelja was a good housewife. He could not deny that. Since the day that she came to live with them, their house had certainly changed for the better. She kept the rooms in good order and had whitewashed the walls and cleaned the windows. Even the animals on the farm were better looked after. The number of calves in the cow sheds had increased. There was more milk. And the meals which she prepared were excellent.

There were plenty of visitors, too. Eventually everyone

in the village had passed through their door. Kazimieras'
brother, who was such a shy fellow by nature, benefited by
this present turn of events and acquired new friends. Anelja
was charming to her guests. Even if they merely caught a
glimpse of her or were the recipients of her smile, they
would return home in high spirits, feeling as if they had
been presented with a gift.

Kazimieras, her husband, was the only one who was
short-changed. Anelja did not smile at him in the way that
she smiled habitually at the guests. She was always serious
with him and indifferent. And Kazys took her attitude very
much to heart, naturally.

Besides this, the relationship between the Šnervas and
the Butkyses changed noticeably. Aunty, who had worked so
hard to make the wedding a success, never liked Anelja;
while Anelja, for her part, showed no interest in Aunty
and was obviously not the person to break the ice between
them. Moreover, she was not in the habit of running in and
out of her neighbors' houses. Neither did she trouble to visit
Aunty. She had no need to visit the Butkyses, for Jonas
was a constant visitor at her house. Just as in the old days,
when Kazys was accepted as a member of the Butkys household, so now Jonas in his turn became a member of the
Šnerva household.

Jonas was constantly in and out of their house, no matter whether good or bad news had brought him there. On
occasions when he found Anelja by herself, he would at once
take both her hands into his in greeting, even if they had
already seen each other on that day. Anelja would smile at
him in a way that seemed to exclude all other people. No,
Anelja did not smile at anyone in the same charming manner
as she did at Jonas. It was little wonder, then, that Jonas
began to long for Anelja more and more. The sun seemed
to shine brightly when he was in her presence. And when he
was away from her, the sky seemed overcast. Jonas grew
dissatisfied and morose.

Aunty, Jonas' mother, was a wise woman. She had always

49

known that Jonas liked girls and that girls liked Jonas. It was time for him to marry, she knew. He had taken such an active part in Kazys' and Anelja's wedding that seemingly, he did not want to leave the happy pair alone now. She was surprised and a little hurt, however, that Jonas did not include her in his confidences any more. As Apolonija thought about it, she realized that Jonas hardly ever spoke to her at all. Often, when he came home from the Šnervas he would go straight to bed, as if he intended to fall asleep at once, but Apolonija would hear him tossing and turning in his bed for a long time. When he did finally fall asleep, however, his sleep was not peaceful. He would sigh and moan. And sometimes he would laugh and cry and suddenly jump up in his bed.

"Jonas, you're suffering from nerves," his mother said to him one day. "Wait, I'll give you some medicine to take."

"Give it to the cats, Mother. They'll like it all right! Plain water is good enough for me; this is no illness." He tried to joke but there was such a sorrowful expression on his face that his mother grew pale as she watched him.

Suddenly, Apolonija seized Jonas' head in both her hands and, looking with anxiety straight into his eyes, she shouted at him, "Jonas, what is the matter with you? Out with it, at once! What is it that you're trying to hide from me?"

Jonas was not equal to such a direct attack. As he looked into his mother's face, something in him collapsed and gave way. Jonas appeared to have lost his mind. His eyes shone strangely and he shouted at his mother like a madman, "Mother! I've sold my soul to the devil!"

Apolonija grew pale all the way to the very tip of her nose. She began to sway back and forth on her feet, then she collapsed in a heap on the floor. She had fainted.

"The Lord have mercy on us!" Jonas exclaimed, quite overcome by this new anxiety which, for the moment, made him forget his former one. He was quite lost and did not know what to do in such an emergency. Fortunately, the maid appeared just then, carrying a bucket of water.

"Good heavens! Has Aunty fainted or something?" Without waiting for an answer, she seized a cup and splashed some water on the old woman's face.

Apolonija came to at once, and Jonas and the maid helped her to her bed. She did not say a word to them and appeared to be very weak. She would not so much as move her hand. They left the room on tiptoe and closed the door.

"Don't you worry about her, now," said the maid. "She'll get over it soon. You'll see. She must have eaten something that disagreed with her. Or perhaps it's some feminine ailment that she's suffering from. You can go now. I'll look after her."

Now that Jonas began to feel a little easier about his mother, his former anxiety, which had upset her so much, returned in full force. It was quite clear to him that his pact with the devil, which he had made some time before, was causing him all this misery and worry.

"Help! Help!" he shouted, and he set off across the fields at a run in his shirt sleeves. In his feverish imagination, he saw vividly the stormy night he had lived through several years before. At that time, he was growing into manhood and his beard was beginning to show. He had invoked the power of the devil; he had promised him his soul on condition that the devil help him to win the woman or girl whom he wanted. From that very night onwards, or so it seemed to Jonas, the devil began to offer him many women. But Jonas showed little interest in them. He even tried to avoid them, until he met Anelja.

He was convinced now that the devil was not going to break off his pact as easily as all that. Perhaps Anelja was his last card, so to speak, and the devil could not wait to seize his soul for himself. Jonas did not want to lose his soul. He hurried across the fields and down the hill to the next parish. He must see the old priest, of whose kindness he had heard so much.

As Jonas ran across the fields, the pewits rose and fell,

whirling about his head and shouting to him as if in greeting: "Living, living, living, living!"

In his excited frame of mind, Jonas took them to be evil spirits who had come to torment him and make fun of him by saying: "We've done our share. We've fulfilled our part of the bargain. Hand over your soul!"

Jonas covered the back of his head with both hands as though attempting to ward off the evil spirits. For some reason he imagined that they could draw out his soul through his head. But when nothing more happened to him, he continued on his way, running through the fields and swamps and splashing mud all over himself. He climbed the hill, descended the other side and walked along the boundary line in the direction of a small village whose wooden church spire had risen into view.

He was on his way to visit a parish where a priest who was about eighty years old lived. The priest's hair was quite gray but he was agile and in full possession of his faculties. Everybody for miles around knew him well since he had lived there for fifty or sixty years. He was well-known for his wisdom and kindness of heart, and the country people brought all their problems to him.

His name was Father Norkus-Norkevičius. It was said that he had been an exceptionally learned man in his youth. He held a graduate degree from the university but a tragedy of one kind or another had occurred in his life just as he was beginning to rise in his career. Suddenly, he found himself to be a person scarcely tolerated in the bishopric, and he was banished to this out-of-the-way place near the marshes where there was not even a main road close by. Probably the very name of the village was unknown to people living any distance from it.

The priest's parishioners were ordinary country folk—regular moles, so to speak. In time, he became one of them. From the day he went to live in the village, Father Norkus never set foot outside his parish except on rare occasions when he was called upon to help out in some other nearby parish. He lived quite forgotten by the outside world. He grew a beard and continued to work in his parish, living on his small income. His expenses were negligible and he had a little money to spare. The country people liked him. They found him to be "an old and wise confessor." Indeed, he was a wise and good-hearted man.

On the day that Jonas was hurrying over to see him, the Reverend Father had already said Mass. He had had his breakfast and was walking up and down in the garden, reading his breviary. The skirts of his home-made cassock swept the path as he moved about.

Father Norkus knew nothing about the village of Puzionys nor had he ever heard of the Šnerva or the Butkys families; and so he was very surprised to see a young man, with his hair standing on end and all spattered with mud, approaching him. He stopped walking and opened his mouth in amazement. Jonas walked straight up to the old priest and seized his hand to kiss it, thereby causing the breviary to fall to the ground. Hurriedly, Jonas bent down to retrieve it and as he was straightening up, he hit his head against the priest's chin. Father Norkus became cross.

"And what might your business be, young man?" said the Reverend Father at last, recovering his equanimity.

Jonas could think of nothing to say but Father Norkus sensed that something was troubling him. Forgetting his aching chin, the priest put his thin old arm across Jonas' shoulders, and miraculously Jonas recovered at once. Then Jonas remembered what had brought him there and his eyes filled with tears.

"I should like to make my confession to you and to no one else, Reverend Father," he said in a whisper with his eyes cast down.

"Why didn't you wait until Friday or Sunday? I always hear confessions on those days," the priest replied.

"Father, I couldn't wait. I thought to myself, *now or never!*"

The priest was about to ask Jonas something else but

thought better of it. Instead, he went into the corridor of his house, unhooked the keys and led Jonas into the little church. There, he pointed to the confessional box and then disappeared into the sacristy.

Jonas attempted to make his confession as best he could.

"Just a minute, just a minute, young man. What has the devil to do with all this?" the priest asked Jonas. "Please listen to me," he went on. "You are a grown man. The Almighty Himself endowed women with beauty and charms to win a husband. For your part, you're a handsome lad, too, you know. You don't need the devil to help you in such matters, I can assure you. It's *youth,* not the devil, that brings the aches and pains of falling in love. But I can see from your face, young man, that your present condition is not enviable. It's time for you to marry, that's all I can say. Are you in love with anyone?"

"I am, Father. She's a wonderful girl, too," Jonas said, whispering passionately into the confessional with his mouth glued to the railings.

"Oh, I'm glad to hear it. Then you've nothing to worry about. If you love each other enough now, it will last you all your married life. But you must ask for the Church's blessing."

"Father, I . . . I think I had better explain. She's already had the blessing . . . with another man."

"Oh, that's bad. I don't like the sound of it at all. Have you both broken the pledge given to her husband?"

"God forbid—no! She's the wife of my very best friend, who's closer to me than a brother."

"That's all right, then. Perhaps you only love her, without desiring her. Some people call that Platonic love, or loving a person from afar, so to speak."

Jonas could not distinguish between "loving" and "desiring"; what he felt for Anelja was all the same to him. He had not realized until now that he could have been accused of wanting to take Anelja away from her lawful husband.

"Well?" the priest asked.

54

"I don't know, Father. I only know that she's always in my thoughts, day and night. She likes me, too, you know. It's as though she was offering me her heart and soul. How will it all end, do you suppose, Father?"

"In a catastrophe, of course. It's very wrong to feel like that, you know. You're committing mortal sin. My son, you're breaking the sixth and the ninth commandments."

"Father, her husband Kazimieras is such a close friend of mine."

"There you are! In this case, you're going to hurt your closest friend as well as the Good Lord."

"Help me, then, Father!"

"It won't be easy for you. You'll have to come to terms with yourself. Young man, you can't do it without God's help and the help of His Holy Mother. If you want them to strengthen you, then you must first show that you're in the right disposition not to sin further—which means that you must not go and see the woman in question any more. You must not even look in her direction until the danger has passed. And you must be truly sorry for your sinful thoughts. For your penance, recite the Litany of the Sacred Heart in this church, lying crosswise in front of the altar. Don't worry, nobody will see you here."

As soon as the priest rose, Jonas seized him by the legs and embraced him, pressing his face against the black cloth and kissing it. Then he smote his breast so loudly that the little church resounded. "Have pity on me," he cried. "Have pity on me, a miserable sinner, Oh Lord!"

When at last Jonas was ready to leave, the priest made the sign of the cross over him. He followed Jonas with his eyes for a long, long time until Jonas disappeared completely out of sight. Then he sat down on a bench in the sun, lost in thought. He sat still, as if paralyzed. The maid called to him once or twice but he did not hear her. Nor did he see his favorite dog, which came up to him to be stroked. The tragedy of his own life suddenly rose before his eyes like an episode in a film and he saw all its consequences.

His intellectual career, which he had had to give up; his banishment to this remote corner of the world, where the tasks which he had to perform were far below his abilities and talents; all these misfortunes had resulted from his own love for a woman!

✓   ✓   ✓

On his return home, Jonas found his mother feeling a little better. He kissed her warmly and told her where he had been.

"I'm so glad you've been to see the Reverend Father, Jonas. May the Holy Mother of God keep you safely in her care!"

From that day onwards, Jonas was not to be seen at the Šnerva house any more. Nor did the Šnerva family come to visit his home. All ties seemed to have been broken, as if with an axe. But Jonas was still not at peace with himself. Thoughts of Anelja gnawed at his heart day and night. All the joy that he had felt before, now disappeared completely. He took to walking about unshaven for weeks at a stretch, looking like some haggard old man. Even when he did shave, he didn't look much better: there were dark circles around his eyes, and his face appeared pale and drawn.

Anelja never mentioned Jonas; one would have thought that he had never existed. But she grew thin and pale, too. The neighbors said that she would recover her looks in no time at all. They whispered among themselves that she was expecting a child. But Kazimieras knew better. Sometimes she would stand for hours at the window, watching the Butkys yard. When she saw Jonas coming out of the house, she would merely raise her eyebrows. Anelja could tell, however, that Jonas was suffering as much as she. How he had changed! He was no longer the gay and carefree "matchmaker" whom she had met at her parents' home for the first time. But he was just as dear to her as he had been before.

Kazimieras' wife, Anelja, had given her heart so completely to Jonas that she was scarcely aware of the presence of her husband. Kazimieras, for his part, had always known that from the beginning Anelja had liked Jonas better than she liked him. But he had not paid much attention to this fact and had hoped that Anelja's feelings towards him would change after her marriage. He did not want to blame Anelja; he held Jonas responsible for everything that had gone wrong. They did not speak about Jonas when they were alone. This seemed worse than if they had talked about him all the time. It was clear to Kazys, however, that neither of them would have spoken about him without emotion.

Before she went to bed, Anelja would kneel for a long time in the darkness with her rosary in her hands. Was she praying for Jonas, for Kazys or for herself? Nobody knew. She would go into their bedroom only when Kazimieras was snoring, or pretending to be asleep. He felt sorry for Anelja. He could see that she was suffering a great deal by trying to remain faithful to him.

Kazimieras also grew thin and haggard-looking, and his hatred for his old friend, Jonas, increased with each new day. He had been such a fast friend all his life! But now, because of his love for Anelja, Jonas was wrecking all their lives. Kazys wondered whether Jonas, the person most to blame, was suffering too.

SIN AT EASTER

KAZYS AND ANELJA continued to live with each other in this unhappy fashion. How could matters have improved while Jonas stayed in such close proximity to them? However, there is an end to everything.

The atmosphere in the Šnerva household had grown very sad. Little by little, the young people had stopped calling since Anelja no longer greeted anyone with pleasure. The competition between Aunty and Anelja for first place in the village was abandoned, and even Aunty's popularity declined somewhat because of Jonas' unhappiness and the anxiety she felt for him. In the evenings, on the other side of the street, Anelja's shadow could be seen kneeling on the threshold of the granary; the owner of the shadow was responsible for all the misfortune. Like St. Monica, Apolonija knelt in tears and in prayer at the threshold of her own granary, weeping for her son. The sky clouded over above both households. There was no sun and the air grew oppressive, as before a storm.

The whole of Lent passed in this manner and a late Easter was fast approaching. Although in this first half of April no buds had appeared on the trees, everything was in readiness for the flowering of spring. The temperature would rise sharply on sunny afternoons but the nights were still cold. The pewits had announced their presence some time earlier in the marshes and now the larks sang in the air as if anxious to make up for lost time. Ploughing had begun in preparation for the summer crops, and sowing, too, was in progress in some fields. Women took great pleasure in the newly hatched goslings, and the geese made loud, protesting noises when their owners tried to shut them up in their pens.

When the Easter confession was behind them, everybody began to feel more cheerful. Even the dark mood of the Šnerva and Butkys households grew a little lighter.

Anelja colored a large bowlful of eggs by boiling them in a pot with onion skins, and she cooked a large ham. She spent a long time cleaning her house before Easter since she had somewhat neglected her household duties of late. After the storm windows had been taken out, the rooms became much lighter and gave quite a different appearance to the house. With the approach of Easter and of spring, everyone's spirits rose and their blood began to run faster. Even Kazys' face, which had grown thin and sallow from anguish and from fasting, brightened a little.

Late in the afternoon on Holy Saturday, there was

58

scarcely a soul to be found at home in the village. Most people had set off for church in order to take part in the solemn watch over the tomb of Christ and to be in good time for the joyful Mass of the Resurrection, which was to take place very early in the morning, at sunrise. Only Kazys and his wife had stayed behind. The farmer's duty in that part of Lithuania, his way of honoring the family, was to rise very early on Easter morning and drive to church in a large gig in order to bring the family safely home. The mistress of the house would stay behind to set the milk to boil and put the finishing touches on the lavish Easter breakfast which followed the seven weeks of fasting.

The village people of Puzionys, from the youngest to the oldest, took their fasting very seriously so that Easter morning was very meaningful to them from a physical as well as a spiritual point of view. The Resurrection of Christ was an ever-recurring fact to them, not merely some mystical ritual. On Holy Saturday, these country people kept watch over the grave of their crucified Christ, who was to rise again on Easter morning. At that time, they would walk around the church three times in procession singing *Alleluja,* the church bells would peal loudly and a volley of shots would be fired, just as in the old days when the town was about to be attacked by the Swedes. There were tears of joy in their eyes as they sang hymns because Christ, Who had conquered sin and even death itself, had risen.

Easter morning is perhaps the only time of the year when people feel really clean in spirit and free from all sin. It is almost as if they have risen above all earthly things at last.

Apolonija, who had prepared her Easter table well in advance, set off for church on foot on Holy Saturday together with the rest of her household. Jonas was left quite alone in the house. He was to drive over in the chilly hours of Easter morning and bring them all back.

Now it was evening and everything had grown very quiet. Not a dog barked and there was not a sound anywhere. The village was like a cemetery. And there was frost in the air.

But with the coming of dawn, the village men began to stir. They harnessed the horses and drove off to bring their families back from church. Kazys Šnerva was among them. As he left his yard and turned into the village street, he noticed that Jonas' horse and cart stood in readiness.

Jonas would be the last one to leave. But it was still early and his horse was a fast one. In any case the villagers of Puzionys always left home a good hour too early. But this was not the reason Jonas had lingered behind. Usually, he was the first to leave home on Easter morning. But he had not slept all night and he was feeling drowsy. Now he found himself gazing at the Šnerva house without realizing what he was doing. Just then, Anelja appeared in the doorway. She was not dressed in her Sunday clothes; it must have been her turn to stay at home. Jonas stood rooted to the ground as if he were paralyzed.

For the first time in many months, he failed to keep his promise—the promise that he had made to old Father Norkus that he would not even look in the direction of Kazys' wife. As soon as he caught sight of Anelja, Jonas could not take his eyes off her. And Anelja, for her part, was unable to look away from Jonas. Her eyes were full of longing. It was a longing, however, not of an active but of a passive kind, which draws the other person like a magnet. Perhaps strong feelings of this sort, feelings which clouded the understanding and judgment, and which destroyed the will, were truly the "work of the devil."

Jonas was quick to notice the expression in Anelja's eyes, even from the distance that separated them. Her eyes struck him as being very large and full of enchantment. But there were dark shadows beneath them, he noticed. He ran across the street as swiftly as a fox. Scarcely a minute had passed before they found themselves inside the house and in each other's arms, locked in a firm embrace. It was as if no power in the world could separate them. They kissed and embraced, taking such delight in each other that one would have thought that they had been lost to each other seemingly forever and had suddenly discovered each other again. From time to time they drew back and examined each other's faces and eyes as if to make sure that it was really they, Jonas and Anelja, who were standing there and not someone else. Then they would kiss each other again. Scarcely knowing himself what he was doing, Jonas carried Anelja about in his arms, now up and down the corridor, now across the living room, as if he was unable to find a place where he could put her down safely. It seemed to him now that Anelja was like a continuation of his own body and that she could not be separated from him.

Anelja had almost fainted with joy, and Jonas was seized as if by madness. The two were caught and held by a whirlwind of love and were oblivious of everything that went on around them. Neither of them had tasted such bliss in all their lives. Only with the coming of the morning, when the sun had risen and Easter bells began to ring in the distance along with the sound of the cannonade echoing in the windowpanes, did Anelja realize what had happened.

"Dear God, it must be the very time of the Resurrection! What have we done, oh what have we done!" she exclaimed wringing her hands, and she hurried out towards the barn.

The first thought that came to her was that she must hang herself in the barn. She tried the door, but it was locked. Then she ran into the shed, but she could not find a piece of rope anywhere. Suddenly, she felt overcome and she collapsed helplessly on the floor.

"At the very time of the Resurrection. . . . At the very time of the Resurrection!" Jonas kept muttering to himself in a dull, hoarse voice. It was as if not he but someone else was speaking. He hurried back into his yard where his horse stood harnessed and ready, seated himself in the cart and whipped the animal smartly across the back. The poor frightened beast trotted nervously into the street and started

61

galloping off in the opposite direction from where the Easter Mass was being said.

Feeling the sharpness of Jonas' whip on his flanks, the horse rushed swiftly ahead. Jonas, in his overwrought state of mind, imagined that the devil had seized him at long last and was carrying him off to hell with all possible speed. Surely, in a few seconds, his journey would be over. Jonas lay in a heap on the floor of the cart, awaiting his terrible fate.

At long last, the horse, foaming at the mouth and completely exhausted, stopped at the churchyard of the Reverend Norkus. The animal had covered a ten-kilometer circle around the valley.

There was not a soul about—everyone had gone home. Slowly, Jonas came to himself. He recognized the place and then remembered what had happened. The enormous consequences of his sin rose before him all at once and he felt that it was useless to look for help. He did not want to see the old priest. How could the Reverend Father help him now, when Jonas had broken his pledge? But to go home? How could he go home? They would have found out everything by this time. And they would have passed judgment on him. How could he face his old friend, Kazys, or his mother? Or the people of the village, for that matter?

He drove off, hoping that his horse would take him anywhere but to the village of Puzionys. He did not urge the horse on this time, but instead allowed it to run at its own pace. Slowly, the day was drawing to a close. The sun was setting and little by little, it began to grow dark. Jonas did not know what time it was or where he was. Finally, he lifted his head and looked about him. The horse had carried him into a yard, then stopped and neighed with pleasure. The animal had brought him home.

✓   ✓   ✓

Kazimieras was the first to hurry back on that Easter morning. He had gone around the church in procession as usual, but all the time he had felt uneasy. When his heart seemed to have stopped beating for a moment, he knew that something dreadful had happened at home. Either the house was on fire or an equally frightening calamity had taken place. All the joy of Easter left him and he grew very alarmed. He could scarcely contain himself until he reached his wagon, and then he drove home as fast as he could.

He left his horse standing in the yard and rushed into the house. There was no one there, and it was cold in the living room. The fire had not been lit. Anelja was nowhere to be found, neither in the parlor nor in the bedroom nor in the storehouse.

She has run away with Jonas, Kazimieras thought to himself. He could not remember having seen Jonas in the church.

Or she has made an end of herself, he thought anxiously. He ran across to the open shed and there he found Anelja kneeling on the floor in an awkward position.

"Anelja, little one! What is wrong? Are you ill or something?" He spoke to her as a father to his child who had suddenly been taken ill.

He lifted her up in his arms and carried her into the house. Then Anelja opened her eyes slowly and looked carefully at her husband. She was astonished at the expression she saw on his face. It was full of love and anxiety and pity for her. Anelja was very moved. She pressed her face to his and began to weep in a desperate manner.

"Tell me, Anelja, what has happened to you? Has anybody harmed you in any way?" Kazimieras asked.

"My dearest husband, my God-given one. . . . At the very time of the Resurrection, when the church bells were ringing out . . . Jonas and I. . . ."

Kazimieras understood. He grew pale as a corpse, then reddened as if all his blood had rushed to his face. He put Anelja to bed, covered her up with blankets and closed the door quietly. Then he went straight into the barn to rummage among some old pieces of iron in a box there. He chose one that best suited his purpose and then hurried towards the Butkys farm. He was looking for Jonas.

The house was empty and there was no sign of either Jonas or his mother anywhere. Where were they? he wondered.

Just you wait, my friend! he said to himself. I'll repay you for all the harm you've done . . . just as you've repaid me for my lifelong friendship with you by wrecking my life and Anelja's.

Kazys decided to wait until they returned. He paced back and forth in the yard like a caged animal, and when a good hour had passed, he saw Aunty coming home on foot with the others. Where was Jonas? Kazys hurried out to meet them.

"Where is Jonas?" he demanded.

"How am I to know?" replied Apolonija, looking anxious and concerned. "As you know, he ought to have come to fetch us a long time ago." She searched the house and the farm buildings but to no purpose. Jonas had clearly left home. There was no horse and no wagon to be found anywhere. Where could he have gone? By the look on Kazys' face, Apolonija could tell that something had happened. She grew even more alarmed.

She went into the parlor and knelt down before the cross. "Christ, newly risen today, save my child!" she implored.

When she rose to her feet at last, Apolonija walked over and sat down near the window. Even when it had grown dark and everyone had gone to bed, she remained sitting there like a statue, waiting for her son to return. It seemed like the longest day in her whole life.

At last, Jonas came home. As soon as Apolonija looked at her son's face, she knew what she wanted to know. There was no need for words.

✓   ✓   ✓

As the days passed by, Kazimieras did not forget his plan to take revenge on Jonas. He was a grown man, after all, and not some shepherd boy to be trifled with. But even the soul-shattering events that had taken place on Easter day had not cured him of his love for Anelja.

Jonas was not long in regaining his composure. He did not have the slightest wish to leave his village any more. Nobody could have forced him to do so, even if they had tried. Nothing mattered to him any more—neither his mother, nor the village gossips, nor Kazimieras himself, for that matter. All he wanted was to be close to Anelja, come what may. Yes, even if his soul were to fall into the hands of the devil, such was the strength of his feeling for her.

As soon as Jonas heard that Anelja was feeling better and that she had overcome her nervous shock, he was full of longing for her. He longed to be with her again, to see her, to kiss her, and to be happy with her as he had been in those early hours of Easter morning. He went on tormenting himself in this fashion day after day. He was ready to do anything in order to gain Anelja for himself. Not for a moment did it occur to him to ask what Anelja would have said to such a suggestion. It did not occur to him that Anelja, who had succumbed to her feelings once, would perhaps be strong enough to resist him in the future. He could not imagine that Anelja would ever change in her feelings for him. His plan to win her for himself was always at the back of his mind.

In the end, it was Kazimieras and not Jonas who brought matters to a head. Kazys Šnerva made no further attempt to talk to Anelja about what had taken place between her and Jonas. But when he went to bed at night, he could not sleep. He had forgiven Anelja her weakness, but how could he be sure that Jonas would not try to win her for himself yet again? No one in the whole world could have given him this assurance, and he could not go on living with doubt.

One market day, Kazimieras saw Jonas crossing the yard and he called to him, "Jonas, let's go and talk things over.

How much longer do you suppose we can go on living like this?"

Jonas glanced at Kazimieras' face and froze. But at the same time he welcomed the opportunity of coming to some sort of a solution. Hadn't he been waiting for just such an opening himself? Without saying anything, he put on his jacket and walked over to the other yard. Then he and Kazimieras drove off.

Instead of keeping to the main road, which would have taken them to the town, Kazimieras drove past the highway and began to descend into the valley known as Pewit Valley.

There was a saying at Puzionys that just as a ploughman cannot live separated from the soil, likewise the pewits could not exist without the marshes. Jonas and Kazys were children of nature. They worked hard in the fields, but when they wanted to enjoy themselves a little, they went to the Pewit Valley.

The valley was several kilometers wide. It was down here that the water collected from all the surrounding fields and a small brook carried it to a larger river. Except for the running brook, however, the valley was all marshland where sedge and many other varieties of grasses grew. These were of little use to the country people or their animals. It was a place of mounds and hillocks, where layers of peat were in formation. Certainly the land would be very valuable in the future, but in the meantime it was neither good for ploughing nor as pasture land. The cranes used it as their breeding ground, but even they did not seem to like it very much.

A small forest of deciduous trees flourished on higher ground nearby, adding beauty to the marshland. Birch trees, alder trees and nut trees grew there. It was said that long ago, lime trees were to be found there, also, but when they were still young saplings, goats destroyed them by gnawing on them and trampling them down. The village people came to the Pewit Valley in the winter, when they were short of wood, or in the summer, when they brought their horses

66

there to graze. In the spring and fall, the place was deserted except for the birds which were very much at home in the valley. Jacksnipe, hoopers, wild duck and other marshland birds abounded. However, the pewits exceeded them all in number. The pewits, so to speak, had claimed the territory of the marshes for themselves and had given it its own atmosphere. Kazys and Jonas had known and liked the Pewit Valley well, ever since they were small boys.

❧   ❧   ❧

In the early spring, when they were youngsters, Kazys would say to Jonas, "Jonas, do you know that that awkward, owlish boy who works on Gimbutas' farm has already brought home pocketfuls of pewit eggs? Enough to make an omelette for the whole family? He wants to get a few slices of bacon from Mrs. Gimbutas, though. Ah, she'll give him some, no doubt, in the end. What are we waiting for? Let's go on Sunday."

"Nest robbing? Are you mad? We're much too old for that, now," Jonas would reply disdainfully, for the sake of form, while his heart was beating fast with joy.

"Well, let's go hunting, then, if you don't want to look for eggs," Kazys would say then, knowing full well that neither of them had ever owned a gun.

Nevertheless, they enjoyed going to the Pewit Valley very much. They could spend the whole day there, wading through the marshes. They would put on well-oiled boots and set off full of spring fever on the first Sunday in March, directly after coming home from church. They would spend many a happy hour there, jumping from one mound to another and laughing at each other good-naturedly if either of them happened to miss his footing and sink up to his knees in the tar-black mud, while flocks of pewits continued to screech above their heads. If, however, they happened to come across a nest, they would never touch the eggs. The eggs were beautiful, but to touch them was to invite the

67

bird to abandon her nest that year, as the pewit invariably did on scenting an unfamiliar smell.

In any case, the pewits always greeted the two lads as if they were lawbreakers and criminals, and whirled around their heads screeching for all they were worth. They were large, grey-white, speckled birds and were ready to fight against the intruders like half-drunk men in a tavern or like gypsies or irate shopkeepers. In no time at all, they were capable of creating an uproar and tumult, causing dense flocks of neighboring birds to hurry to their assistance.

"Everything belongs to us here! Everything belongs to us here!" they seemed to be saying. "Not until our flock has increased five times shall we go away from this place."

"Do you think they're really afraid of us?" Kazys would say to Jonas, "or are they just playing and making fun of us?" At heart, they felt that the pewits wished them no harm, just as on their part neither Jonas nor Kazys had ever hurt a defenseless bird in their lives. They felt themselves better men, better human beings as a result of this contact with nature. As soon as the sun began to set and the air grew chilly, they would set off for home again and the birds would quiet down until their next visit.

✦   ✦   ✦

What was Kazys thinking, what was he planning to do now, as they drove into the Pewit Valley? Unconsciously, he may have been looking for a satisfactory way out of his predicament.

As they drove over the steep ridge and into the valley, Kazys sat in the wagon lost in thought, with his head bent and one foot thrown out as if in readiness to jump out of the cart. He stared absently at the piece of iron that he had tossed into the wagon before leaving home. He was listening attentively to the music that the pewits were making and, for a moment, at least, he had forgotten all his troubles.

Suddenly, Jonas noticed the piece of iron lying in the

wagon and a thought flashed through his mind: Why, he's going to try and kill me with it!

He was seized with fear and without waiting for further developments, he grabbed the weapon and hit Kazys on the head as hard as he could. One blow would have been sufficient but Jonas could not stop himself from hitting him again and again.

At last he realized what he had done and he began to scream and shout with terror. He tore at his clothes and his hair and started to run away as fast as he could. But his foot caught against a mound and he stumbled and fell.

The pewits began to screech and circle about him. They shouted and quarreled among themselves, almost touching him with their wings.

"Living, living, living!" they called out to him.

Jonas imagined that they were evil spirits. "All right, you've won. I grant you that. You can take me to hell or wherever you wish. There's no place left for me on earth, in any case."

Those were Jonas' last words. But the devil did not haul him off to hell. Instead, Jonas was arrested by the police and sentenced for life to a forced-labor camp in Siberia.

Aunty Apolonija died of a heart attack shortly after she heard the news about her son. As for Anelja, she appeared to have lost her mind. She refused to speak to anyone and would not take any food. Finally, her parents came and took her away with them.

1930

Rimas and Nerimas

Translated by Stepas Zobarskas and Clark Mills

RIMAS AND NERIMAS, two farmers from Augštaičiai, lived across from one another at the very end of the village. Neither was very old, although both had already reached the half-century mark and did not expect to live through another half; both had celebrated their silver wedding anniversaries, too. They were strong and healthy men, hardworking and sober. But, being Lithuanians, they did not overwork themselves as the Latvians did; and on holidays they did not turn down a dram, as fully-pledged teetotalers would have done.

A land survey had established that both farmers owned twenty-five acres of second-class soil, good for cultivation, and over seven acres of useless marshland which they had drained and leveled, and either plowed up or kept for pasture. Since they worked with equal industry, they were also equally rich. The harvests in their granaries were the same; and each had three horses, the likes of which could not have been bought for a hundred rubles. Each also kept ten head of cattle and milked five or six cows—sometimes seven. Yet neither considered dairying as his main occupation; it was only a way to eat well. Each year they sheared an equal number of sheep and slaughtered the same number of pigs. Each kept a flock of geese, too. God only knows whether Providence had intended it as a joke or whether the farmers had arranged it between themselves, but the fact remains that their lives were amazingly alike.

Whenever a child was born to Rimas, one didn't have to

71

wait long for the christening of a Nerimas. And whenever a Nerimas child happened to die, the entire village knew that soon there would be a wake at the Rimas cottage. All told, five children had died in each family and five remained alive: three sons and two daughters.

Their livestock also followed suit: the ewes of both neighbors bore either twins or single lambs. And one day, when Rimas's ewe had given birth to triplets, Nerimas did not even have to visit his barn: he knew that his ewe had also done the same.

The village regarded Rimas and Nerimas as fine men and excellent farmers. Both knew this, and were bashfully proud. They were kind to their neighbors, and helped to settle disputes among them. They were quick to lend a hand in distress and always gave the best advice. No one could tell which was the more generous.

Even the priest could not make a distinction. As far back as the parishioners could remember, the rector had appointed both as elders and entrusted them with the church collections. And whenever, during their pre-Christmas visits, the priests lunched with one of the families, they invariably had to sup with the other.

Both neighbors knew they could not outwit each other, so they tried very hard to keep pace in every small detail. Their intention was not to outdo one another, but to progress at an equal rate.

This competition, the only sore spot in Rimas's and Nerimas's otherwise complacent lives, had swollen and ached for some thirty years until it finally began to create harsh thoughts and unkind feelings.

Being stubborn, both carried unbending differences within their hearts. This was obvious to them, to the village, and to the priests. But it came to nothing, since no one ever mentioned it. They held it to be a private affair between the consciences of the two alone, which were not to be violated.

Rimas and Nerimas allowed their wives and children to remain friendly, so that they ran into each other ten times a day and knew each other's thoughts, words, actions and even designs. But the men never visited each other, never consulted each other, and never spoke to each other, not even to say "Glory be to Jesus Christ," although both were church-goers. If the whole village were assembled at a meeting, even then they tried to express their thoughts through a third person.

"Look, honorable sir, this is how it would seem to Rimas. . . ."

If Rimas decided to move his barn to where his granary stood, the next day found Nerimas tearing the thatch from his barn. If Nerimas started to cut wood to replace his fence, in no time Rimas would be walking towards his own fence and pulling down the old structure. Years before, one of them had repaired the chimney of his smokehouse; the other had done the same. And when one divided his house with partitions for the children and servants, the other did exactly likewise. And it was the same when one enlarged his windows.

The two farmsteads finally looked so much alike that to beggars they presented a kind of divine retribution. These would come to the Nerimases, offer a prayer and receive a piece of bread or some meat. Then they would lower their heads with piety and walk slowly towards the Rimases. Suddenly they would blink their eyes and say:

"Well now, my head must be addled. I was just here!"

And they would return to the Nerimases. Mrs. Nerimas would grow angry and scold them:

"For heaven's sake, you cow (or ox!) " (It depended on the sex of the beggar.) "What's happened to you? Have you started to walk backwards? You've already had your share!"

If Mrs. Rimas scolded the beggars for the same thing she said:

"You sheep (or ram, you!) Have you begun to walk in circles?"

And the beggars would feel embarrassed and curse themselves.

As a matter of fact, the wives and children also competed constantly. If Mrs. Rimas happened to buy her daughters a holiday scarf, the Nerimas girls would fuss about until they received the same gift on the next holiday. If the Nerimas girls were weaving a patterned "Circassian" cloth with silk stripes, then the Rimas girls would do all they could to learn what the stripes were like.

The women and children did not feel it so much, but the men, who had been keeping constant tabs on one another for several decades, were growing tired of this ceaseless and uncontrollable urge to keep up with each other. In fact, their competition had reached the point where one would have been happy to see the other dead.

Undoubtedly, the survivor would have eaten hot cabbage with beef or pork at his neighbor's funeral supper; undoubtedly, he would have refused to go to bed until he had completed the full day of mourning. He would have followed the coffin a good mile and shed tears as it was being lowered into the ground. But, on his way home, he would have repeated the old Lithuanian adage:

"Well, there he is, dead. And he would have lived, if he hadn't died."

Yes, I say, the survivor would certainly have felt some joy in his heart—even though he might not have admitted that a real change had come into his life at last.

✓ ✓ ✓

A keen-sighted man, observing them from a distance, could have noticed several differences between Rimas and Nerimas, of which they themselves were unaware.

Rimas was heavy, of medium height, and constantly sniffing tobacco. Though his cheeks were closely-shaven, his upper lip looked like a smudge of soot. Nerimas was thin, very tall, and he smoked a pipe. When he shaved he left a moustache under his nose; and when his teeth began to fall out, it resembled a shaggy edge of fur.

As for Mrs. Rimas, she was taller than her husband, very

74

handsome and by no means fat. Mrs. Nerimas was short, and although fairly slender, she had such large breasts that whenever she walked or ran she had to support them with both hands.

The Rimas children were dark-skinned like gypsies, with sharp noses and long faces. They were all well-groomed. The Nerimas children were heavy-boned, round-faced, and blunt-nosed, with light hair and blue eyes; their faces looked so bright that one could not help admiring them. The boys looked like girls—their cheeks were so soft, so white and pink.

The Rimas and Nerimas boys were considered the most handsome children in the whole parish. Some preferred the sweet-faced Rimases, others liked the bright-faced Nerimases. All had clear, good voices; but whereas the Rimas boys sang soprano and tenor, the Nerimases sang alto and baritone. The former led and the latter accompanied them; their choir became well known and especially popular at weddings.

When women married in Augštaičiai they brought with them a special quality of their own, a kind of leaven which spread throughout the house.

Mrs. Nerimas was a very sharp, even a hot-tempered woman. Her whole household soon became known for its loud voices and shouting. She had matured early, and at fifteen her breasts had been so firm and pointed that her mother used to say with admiration:

"Such a young girl and already such a cow. . . ."

This nickname stayed with her for the rest of her life. She did not dislike it at home with her parents, and once she had raised her own family, she started to nickname the others:

"Hey, you cow! Hey, you ox!" she would say as the family came together from the fields in the evening. Thus Mrs. Nerimas would punish, halt and warn her "little angels," according to their feminine or masculine sexes.

Even Nerimas got used to saying "Hey you, cow!", shooting the saliva of bitter tobacco through his teeth, when he wanted to chide his wife gently or at least to disagree with her. After all, "cow" was not such an awful word. There was much value in a fat, milk-rich cow. And it did not look so ridiculous; that depended on the end from which one saw it, with its large grass-filled belly, the symmetrical rows of nipples, and its large calm eyes, beautiful, tearful and melancholy. The term "cow" in its most complimentary sense suited Mrs. Nerimas and her youngsters very well indeed.

The dark-haired Mrs. Rimas was even more hot-tempered than Mrs. Nerimas. But she had been well brought up by a quiet mother, and managed to control herself in a very noble way. No one had ever heard her talk louder than necessary. She also knew how to check her anger. When her parents or someone else scolded her, she would not say a word, but simply look at them with her calm little eyes cheerfully, modestly, obediently, like a sheep being led to slaughter.

She was her parents' most beloved child. Even when they scolded her they did so without anger, sweetly. They called her their little sheep; and she liked it. The sheep was a good little animal. It hurt no one; it had no horns, fangs nor claws. It would complain only to God Himself, with a sad, heart-breaking bleat! And look how the ewe loves her lambs! She keeps her eye on them while they eat, and the moment they move away she calls: "Where are you? Don't get lost, come back to your mamma!"

When she married Rimas, who was also soft-spoken and slow, she brought a still calmer spirit into the house. No one ever heard a sound from their yard. They too had arguments, but they could reach an agreement more quickly than others. She took good care of her children; her sweet feminine influence had shaped their hearts and their souls. But when she wanted to punish or scold one of them, she would call out: "Hey you, ewes and rams!"

Sometimes Rimas would observe his wife as she watched her children, filled with her anxiety for them, and then he

76

would mumble with feigned roughness, although he was seething inside with an infinite love, using the word he had borrowed from her:

"You're a real sheep: do you think for a moment that your lambs will disappear?"

And he would continue to inhale tobacco through his nose.

The villagers made no distinction among the individual souls of these two households and never called them anything but "the Nerimas cows and oxen" or "the Rimas ewes and rams." There was nothing insulting or malicious in this, however. People from that region of Lithuania often referred to their women as ewes, for these animals are very much like Lithuanian women, who are humble and do not know how to fight back. They can only cry helplessly: just listen to some of the old folk songs!

✔   ✔   ✔

At least Rimas and Nerimas could compete with each other. The other villagers did not have even this type of diversion. A monotonous, gray life pervaded the village. Everyone was bored and lazy, especially during late autumn. Wearing their fur coats and caps, they sat for hours at their neighbors' tables or just stayed at home. Nothing varied their routine, and they could invent nothing better or more amusing. The gossip monger, the crude flatterer, and the practical joker were esteemed in the village as highly as a good preacher in the church. Even these were not so easy to find, and the villagers seized the slightest occasion to giggle, grin or tease each other. Sometimes the mockery would become a really barbaric affair that ended in death, although it always began without evil intent.

One late spring Rimas's name dominated the talk of the villagers. He had hired a maid, a sloppy spinster named Katré. She bothered no one, and no one bothered her until Rimas's bay horse escaped from the pasture into the Pakalnis village swamp where it enjoyed itself thoroughly in a tract of soft young grass. Now the Pakalnis people cherished this grass more than their own hair, because they had so little of it. One might pull their hair freely on any holiday at the town tavern, but they insisted on being paid for any horse that they caught in their pastures. One had to pay cash as a ransom. In no time they had noticed the Rimases' bay horse and sent their man to seize it and hold it for ransom. But the Rimases' hands, who were working outdoors, had noticed the commotion, too. They had also noticed who was approaching fast. Frightened, they ordered Katré to get the bay horse out of the forbidden pasture before he could grab hold of it.

Katré obeyed and started to run as though someone had set her on fire. But the harder she ran, the more her body waddled. She appeared to be hopping up and down instead of moving forward. Her breasts swayed wildly from side to side like pendulums above her waist, and she could barely place one foot in front of the other. She grew breathless, and by the time she reached the horse she was completely drenched with perspiration. Since the ransomer was now very close, she began to think:

"If I try to lead the horse by hand, he'll hold his ground; if I whip him, he'll stop completely. I'd better climb on and ride him out of the ransomer's grasp. . . ."

The horse was not high, but neither was Katré an expert in Swedish gymnastics. She brushed the horse with her stomach and fell back; she could not manage to seize its mane. She had seen the young boys, even the smallest, reach for the mane with their little hands, then support themselves with the big toe of their left foot against the horse's side, and thus land on top. But Katré tried to get on the horse not from the left side but from the right. She tried to support herself with her right foot, and her toe kept sliding down; she hit her nose against the horse's neck and her eyes became green with anger. Katré cursed and tried to push the horse with her belly. She was now still more wet with perspiration and had completely forgotten the ransomer, so eagerly did she try to straddle the horse, cursing herself for every failure. The ransomer had been standing nearby, watching Katré and laughing with all his might at her fruitless work. The maid was almost ready to faint when she finally heard his voice resounding like some thunderclap from above:

"Stop now and hand your horse to me. I'll mount him faster. Go and tell Rimas that it's useless to send anyone to get him back for less than five *auksinas.*"

He then mounted the horse and rode away.

Five *auksinas!* What will my master say? thought Katré, and suddenly she began to bawl. She did not go straight home through the fields where the hands had been working, but walked back through the village, explaining to everyone that it was not her fault that the horse was so big. . . .

The villagers had watched her labor and had nearly died of laughter; and all of them, as though they had reached an agreement over it, gasped:

"The Rimases' cavalry trooper. . . . The Rimases' cavalry trooper."

The shame was almost too much for Rimas, because of Katré.

"One could kill such a sheep!" cursed Rimas.

He did not kill Katré, however, when she finally returned, nor even punish her. He handed five *auksinas* to his son, forgave Katré her blunders and would soon have forgotten the incident, were it not for his neighbors. Everyone in the village talked of nothing but the "Rimases' cavalry trooper." And did they talk! As soon as someone mentioned "the Rimases' cavalry trooper," all died with laughter. Whenever any of the children encountered a member of the Rimas family, they would tag behind them, barking like puppies:

"The Rimases' cavalry trooper. The Rimases' cavalry trooper!"

The Rimases could hardly go out of their house. And it was most annoying that the Nerimases did not lag behind the others. They laughed leaning against the fence and they laughed at the table as they looked through the window at the Rimas farm. The Rimases saw this, and burned with shame and anger.

All the anger that had been growing in Rimas's heart against the villagers was now directed against Nerimas. He had not seen the others mocking him, but he did see Nerimas. The old conflict added to the outrage. He began to nurse a deadly grudge and desire for revenge. Not even Mrs. Rimas could help. She called him a ram, she laughed, she stroked his hair, she hugged him at night—but to no avail. Rimas became silent; he tossed about in bed and bore ill-will towards everybody. He seemed to be possessed by a devil. Eventually, the entire homestead grew sullen and laughter disappeared.

The devil had sown the seed of wrath even into the hearts of the youngsters. None of them visited the Nerimas youngsters any longer. The Nerimases sensed the reason, and they stopped running to the Rimases.

A week, two weeks passed. The villagers grew bored with the story and stopped laughing. The Nerimas youngsters began to miss their neighbors and felt ashamed of their own mockery. They were about to go and apologize and make it up with Rimas. But old man Nerimas stopped them.

"For such a mere nothing! You'll make them more puffed up than they are now."

Who knows how the comedy might have ended, were it not for another comedy, started by Katré, which turned the villagers' attention in another direction.

One day Katré was walking in the middle of the village street, scratching under her arms. Whatever Katré did, she did with her whole heart, and since all her thoughts were concentrated on how to dig her nails deeper into her armpits, she did not realize that she was about to step on the Nerimases' dog, who lay dozing in the sunshine, right in the middle of the dusty street.

He was a good-for-nothing old dog. Not only had he never bitten anyone in his life, but no one could remember that he had even barked. He was only able to crawl to the table for a crust of bread, and then to lie awkwardly day and night in some cranny. He probably wouldn't have barked even if a murderer were killing his masters, and still less for the neighbors whom he, like the Nerimas family, could not distinguish from himself. But unexpectedly and painfully stepped on in sleep, he jumped and, maddened by fear, grabbed Katré where he could best sink his teeth. He grabbed her softest part and bit into it with gusto. Then he felt ashamed, but not knowing how to apologize, he only bowed his head guiltily, lowered his eyes, and disappeared under a store-house.

Katré began to scream hoarsely from the bottom of her lungs—as only Katré could. With her skirt lifted, she walked through the village explaining to everyone she met how for no reason at all the Nerimases' gray dog had taken a bite out of her.

"All the Nerimases are like their dog," she concluded bitterly.

People began to pour from every yard to see such a rare spectacle. The crowd gathered about Katré, grinned at her, and moved off only when she was about to demonstrate the truth of her words by exposing her injuries.

The more Katré screamed and complained, the more the youngsters laughed; and they felt happy that again some variety had entered their life. They surrounded "Uncle" Mykolas and began to talk about Katré's misfortune. As he could not make head or tail of what they were saying, Mykolas turned towards the comic character herself. Having listened earnestly to her words and still dead-serious, he stroked her aching spot with his large palm and then said:

"It's all right, all right. Nerimas's dog has only kissed you. The Nerimases are all alike—they've been kissing Rimases for a long time. . . ."

After such kind words Katré felt better. She smiled, kissed the uncle's hand and moved towards home, where she soon forgot the whole thing.

81

But the village had not forgotten. "The Nerimases have been kissing Rimases for a long time" clung to their minds, and they doubled over with laughter demonstrating how a Nerimas had kissed Katré and how she had enjoyed that kiss. The crowd first filled the Rimas house and laughed and screamed and giggled; then they descended on the Nerimas homestead.

The Rimases were stunned. Everything had happened so unexpectedly, and a good laugh had not been heard for such a long time that at first they only managed to smile. Only when all the guests had gone did they look at each other's grim faces and suddenly burst into hysterical laughter. Even Mrs. Rimas, who had always known how to control herself, could not stop; and the old man, who seldom ever laughed, joined the company. As they laughed they did not look at Katré, who now felt ashamed. Their eyes were directed towards the Nerimas windows.

Suddenly their hearts felt easier, as though someone had opened a steam valve, letting out the pressure and clearing the air.

Rimas was especially tickled—he who didn't even know how to laugh. He liked the saying enormously. He repeated it with enjoyment, then suddenly fell silent, turned aside and crossed himself; he felt at ease now; his hatred for Nerimas had suddenly fled. His wife glanced at him and understood what was going on in his heart. Overcome with joy, she crossed herself, too.

And thus a happy mood returned to the Rimases; but now the Nerimases were furious. When the Rimases grieved or worried it was not easy to notice, for they were a soft-spoken family. But when the talkative Nerimases became sullen, the whole village knew it.

Now the Nerimas youngsers were angered and refused to visit the Rimas home, while the Rimas children withheld their own visits. The entire force of the anger was concentrated on the Rimases, as if it were their fault alone that the dog had harmed Katré and that the village boys had made such sport of it.

Nerimas felt especially hurt, since for a while he had risen head and shoulders above Rimas; and now suddenly, in the twinkling of an eye, he had fallen into an abyss. From his own deep hole he could scarcely notice that those he had formerly ridiculed were now happy and laughing at him instead.

Laughing at him! This was something he had never experienced in his long life—that anyone could have dared to make fun of him. And he began to nurse such vengeful feelings against Rimas that he could not sleep at night. He became as dour as Rimas had been before, and he remained so for nearly a month.

The gray dust of life rose, as if a hen had scratched the ground; and it obscured the light, both human and divine.

✓ ✓ ✓

One autumn the Rimases and Nerimases sent their second oldest sons to the army. They knew that life would become harder, for the old masters would have to guide their ploughs themselves. Luckily, during the period between Christmas and Lent, their eldest sons returned from service. After the return of these two strong ploughmen, the neighbors did not miss the others so much.

One day, in the midst of the harvest season, a foreman wearing a hastily-attached badge on his rumpled and ragged cap ran up to Rimas and Nerimas and announced breathlessly:

"Mobilization! The youngest men in the reserves must be ready by tomorrow—they probably won't come back." Then he ran on.

The village was frightened. Almost every home had a farmer-soldier. So many would be missing! All the plans for the coming fall and winter would collapse. Now there would be no telling how many would marry, or how many farms would obtain new hands. The girls who had sweethearts or who still awaited their ideal princes began to cry. But the older people's wives, who already had a flock of children, cried even more. In such cases they would remain mistresses and masters in solitude. There were also as many wives of artisans, whose husbands' work was their only source of bread. They could not find tears enough to bemoan the calamity.

But all farm worries were at last put aside, and the only concern became the war itself. There would be battles, shooting, bombs, cannons and machine-guns; there would be stabbing with bayonets—how could anybody remain alive? Would he return or not—yours sweetheart, and yours wife or mother?

No one could remember such a troubled evening as that of July 18, 1914. No one wanted to go to bed, yet there was little to talk about. Everyone's head and heart were filled only with the thought and dread of the war. Since no one had any idea of what war meant, they could only gnaw their lips, lament and spill meaningless words.

"See what has happened—oh, what shall we do now?" And this went on endlessly.

At last, reluctantly, they dispersed through their *klétis and seklyčias* to sleep. But there was no rest even in bed.

Neither Mrs. Rimas nor Mrs. Nerimas could fall asleep. First one and then the other would walk out of her *klétis* and pretend to look around, to see how high the Pleiades had risen or the Great Bear and Orion. They could not sleep; they felt an urge to pray or to cry, so anguished were their hearts. All their beloved stars twinkled as before. And there were so many that one wanted to pick them. It was the beautiful sky of a Lithuanian summer night, beautiful as it is usually only in winter. But no one could enjoy that night. The two neighbors did not look up at the sky; they glanced toward one another. Something moved deep in the hollow of their throats, and suddenly they felt short of breath, as if someone were choking them. They tottered and fell, not on the ground but into each other's arms. They held

84

each other by the shoulders, pressed their breasts, swayed to both sides, and burst out crying. They sobbed and trembled spasmodically, but said nothing; they needed no words. Everything was clear: each had a son in the army already, and now two more sons would have to go. Words were but streaks of pain, and their tears washed all the streaks away. In the middle of the road their two sorrows blended like two white ash-trees for which the world had become too narrow, too tight for life. For them the world and space had vanished. They felt that they had to embrace one another, since misfortune always seeks its companion and the solace it offers. They felt that they, who had needed one another for so many years, did so now most of all, with their unhappiness at hand. They realized how small and unimportant were the trivialities of life in which some people found joy and others chagrin.

They parted as good friends. No one had seen this scene on the road, and in the morning the events of the night before seemed as vague as a dream. If only they had had time to think it over they would have recognized the real fruit of their meeting: not the least trace of neighborly anger, mockery, or pretentiousness was left in their hearts.

Early in the morning, before the cattle had left for the pasture, the two mothers, Niobes both, prepared their soldiers—Mrs. Rimas her "ram" and Mrs. Nerimas her "ox." They had tried to conquer their feelings, and it seemed at first that no torture could have pressed one tear from their eyes. But the moment they looked at their boys, both straight as candles, both still recalling their military training and discipline and pacing to and fro with light, strong steps, something burst in the women's breasts and the tears began to flow again.

The village liked these soldiers more than any of the other "horned livestock." There was a reason for this. Before the Rimas and Nerimas youngsters had gone into the service, they had graduated from the public school. They were smart and quick, and after four years they had returned as head sergeants. Neither took pride in the three stripes on their sleeves, nor in the gold decorations they had received for their service. They remained the same villagers they had always been, with the same feelings as the other villagers.

The only difference was that during the period of their military service they had learned to read better and to understand what was printed in the newspapers. In fact, they brought back with them the first newspapers to have been seen in the village for a long time: young Rimas favoring the "clerical" newspaper and young Nerimas the "anticlerical." To the ignorant village these two had brought with them a breath of fresh air.

As soon as they had time to spare, they gathered in the lads' homes hoping to find out what other Lithuanians were doing in the big world outside, and to learn more and more about the kings who had grown angry among themselves. For once they had lost interest in the ridiculous, empty affairs of the village.

During the times of hard work they forgot the newspapers and tried to play tricks on the "smart ones." But now, with misfortune on their heads, everyone hurried to ask forgiveness for what they might have done to hurt them, and to plead from the bottom of their hearts:

"Come back healthy and as soon as you can. We will be waiting for you!"

The crowds wandered from the Nerimases to the Rimases and back again. Only the hosts did not mingle among themselves. Alone, they hitched their carts to take their youngsters to the county seat. Neither the soldiers nor their parents said a word to one another. Even those who remained at home made no effort to settle their own differences. They faced great things and had forgotten the less significant but at least they had stopped gossiping about each other.

They never spoke of those who had left, but kept silent as one often does about the dead. Sometimes they seemed to forget them when no news came for a month or two.

One day a postcard awakened the feelings that were at

last beginning to weaken. Accidentally or by design, it was addressed to Rimas and Nerimas in Augštaičiai, Kaunas Government. It bore no date and no sign from where it had come—not even a stamp or cancellation. It was marked only: "From the active military service." The message looked even stranger: it had been written by the Rimas boy, but had been signed by both.

"Our beloved ones," it read. "If you love us, pray for us. We are in the line of fire. We fight and advance and fight again, pushing our enemy back. So far we've been lucky; we conquer the enemy, although many, many have been lost on our side. Thank God, we are not yet seriously wounded, but we are bruised and tired. We fight bravely. Our superiors know this and have promoted us to junior officers for the duration of the war. The end seems far away. Please pray to God that we live to see it."

Rimas's daughter received the postcard at the Post Office. She almost lost her head with joy as she read it. In the entire text she had noticed only one line: that the boys who had left home as sergeants would return as officers, with beautifully ornamented coats and narrow pants, with spurs and swords that touched the ground.

When she met her counterpart on the Nerimas side, she seized her, kissed her, swung her around, and read the letter aloud. Then she ran home as quickly as her legs could carry to announce the news to her parents. She told everyone she met that her brother had become almost a general. The news reached the other Rimas youngsters, who happened to be in town. All became so excited that they did not wait for vespers. Both the Rimases and Nerimases began to pursue the girl with the letter.

They could not catch up with her, but on the road they became friends again. At first both parties felt embarrassed, though none felt any hatred toward the others. Only, having avoided each other for such a long time, it was hard to act as they had before. Both groups pretended to think only of their brothers who had become—of all things!—officers. . . .

Talking about them the whole way in loud voices, they rushed headlong into the Rimas homestead and shouted:

"Our brothers have become generals!"

Suddenly they fell silent: they had come at the very moment that the pious Mrs. Rimas, who had already heard from two sources that the boys were alive, had fallen to her knees with her eyes and hands uplifted in prayer.

"Thank you, most holy Virgin, for hearing our prayers and for watching over our children. . . ."

She said "our children," having no doubt that Mrs. Nerimas had also prayed every morning and evening for both of them.

She had scarcely risen before the youngsters ran with the letter to the Nerimas house.

"Dear aunt, look what beautiful news we have!" exclaimed Rimas's daughter, and began to read.

Nerimas's son snatched the letter, but his sister pulled it away. At last, spelling out word by word, as though it were a boring task performed for someone else and not themselves, they began again to read. In the meantime Rimas's son dashed home.

Now Mrs. Rimas said she did not quite understand about their becoming officers, and asked to hear the letter once more.

All three children ran to get it. They met old Nerimas in the yard and immediately kissed his hand. Nerimas was taken aback for a moment, but his face beamed. He went into the house happy; he had already heard the news in town.

By the time he unharnessed his horse and came into the house, Rimas's boys had already left with the letter. He wanted to hear the news with his own ears, from the original text, which the village had elevated into a real newspaper. Before he could express his wish, his boys ran off to the Rimases for the letter.

The villagers, who wanted to share the good news, arrived later.

Gradually the life of the two neighbors returned to its earlier routine: ten times a day the children would run from one house to the other. Finally the two mothers met on the road, kissed each another, smiled and shed a tear of joy. Both agreed to drive to the parish house the next day, to have a Mass said for their boys.

The rector, who knew about the chilled relations of the neighbors, was surprised and even disheartened when he saw the two women arriving together.

No doubt to complain against each other, he thought. But he changed his mind as soon as he noticed the expressions on their faces: there was not a trace of anger left.

Both women held three rubles in their hands, and both tried to explain at once, now and then showing him the postcard to add weight to their words.

The rector took the postcard, asked the women to sit down, read it silently, thought for a while, then took their money, opened his desk and laid two silver coins in front of each of them.

"What is that, Father?" asked Mrs. Nerimas.

"We wanted a solemn mass," added Mrs. Rimas softly.

"I understand," the rector assured them. "And it will be a solemn high mass. We'll light all the altar candles. But it has to be a joint mass, one for both: this is your children's wish. You see, they wrote one letter to both of you and sent it to one address. They want all of you to pray for them. We must honor their request."

Only now did the women see why their sons had written and sent the letter in such a strange way. They knew now that their soldiers had made peace and that they were as clever as the rector himself. They had brought their peace to those who remained at home.

The women were overjoyed.

"Let it be as you say, Father: have one mass to offer our thanks to God and another to ask the blessing of His mercy on our children in the days to come," said Mrs. Rimas, and both women returned the silver coins to the rector.

When the first mass was offered, both the Rimases and Nerimases rode in their large wagons to the church. They prayed with ardor and piety, and none separated the two soldiers in their minds. Together, the two mothers gave alms to the beggar, who did not fail to pray for the intention of their boys.

"Pray for our children Rimas and Nerimas."

They repeated the same thing the following Sunday.

On the way to church and back, the Nerimas youngsters crowded into old Rimas's wagon, and the Rimas children jumped in with the Nerimases. And all of them chattered, their beautiful, honest, friendly faces bringing calm and peace into the old men's hearts.

✦　　✦　　✦

From that moment harmony returned again, and the autumn harvesting became a happy affair. Once more, the Rimas and Nerimas families did everything together. Even on occasions when they were forced to labor separately, the family that finished first ran over to help the other.

Old Rimas and Nerimas, alone, did not seem to have changed. True, they were now able to sleep nights; they no longer cast ugly glances at each other; sometimes they even forgot their rivalry. Nevertheless, they did not visit one another, nor did they speak. They felt no need for it.

Meanwhile, their sons fought on. In the same regiment and unit, they had taken their hot food from one field kitchen and marched day after day after day together. Often they faced death. These two friends of old had long since forgotten the small village accident that had damaged so many fine feelings. Within a few days they acted like close acquintances, but not yet as comrades and brothers.

One day they were sent on reconnaissance duty. When they set out there were many soldiers together, but as they advanced they separated to form a loose "net" that covered several miles. Thus they moved ahead, so as to trap the enemy in one of their meshes.

Rimas was riding about a half-mile away from Nerimas. Suddenly he spotted a group of enemy scouts who had noticed Nerimas and were pursuing him on horseback. Nerimas opened fire. Rimas's heart was paralyzed with fear; it almost stopped beating. The enemy had not yet noticed him. With each enemy shot he closed his eyes and then opened them to see whether Nerimas was still astride his horse. Every shot pierced his heart as if he himself had been hit.

This feeling did not last long. Rimas gritted his teeth, pressed his gun to his shoulder and aimed at an enemy scout who was approaching Nerimas at enormous speed. He fired and thrust at the air with the barrel of his gun at the same time, as if to pierce the enemy with a bayonet. He was so sure of his shot that he did not even look to see whether the enemy had fallen from his horse. He then defended his flanks and rear, firing his rifle and revolver.

The enemy soldiers saw that they were trapped between two fires. So did Nerimas, who knew he had been saved by one of his own comrades. He counter-attacked his pursuers and both fought like madmen, with loud shouts. The enemy soldiers took fright: two fell to the ground wounded, another two fled. A fifth was killed instantly by a bullet from Rimas.

The friends rode up to the injured, removed their weapons and, ignoring their pleas for mercy, fell into each other's arms. Rimas began to weep—so great were his tension and relief.

"Are you safe? Are you sure you haven't been hit?" he asked, looking at Nerimas with anxious affection.

Nerimas's lips trembled; he pressed Rimas against his chest and said:

"So—you felt concerned about me!"

"Only now do I realize how close you were to me. I was more worried about you than myself, my friend."

And it was now clear that, born together in one heap, they had grown as if within one heart—that the dust of life might darken but could never change them. All the bitter enmities of the past had been false and shaped out of the feelings of their parents.

The two friends never parted thereafter. Wherever one volunteered to go, the other followed, and was more afraid for his friend than for himself. In battle they tried to protect each other. They shared their food and, at night, covered each other with their blankets. The whole unit knew of their friendship, and the soldiers chaffed them; but when they were alone, they admired the two Lithuanians "who loved each other like two girls."

A month passed. In one battle, all the officers of the regiment were killed. The two friends took over the command and completed what the officers had begun; their superiors commended them for bravery and made them junior officers for the duration. This was the news that they had sent on to their families. To write about their reconciliation had not come into their minds; it was such a foolish triviality, not worth mentioning. The wonderful sign of their unity had appeared in the form of the card and had accomplished much more than words ever could. It had united those who were left behind.

The friends received little news from home, although their families wrote as soon as they had a sign that they were alive. But even the few lines that they read showed that relations at home had become as open and warm as their own. Poor fellows, little did they know how dearly they would have to pay before an animosity that had lasted a quarter of a century was completely destroyed.

✓   ✓   ✓

One morning Nerimas was awakened by a scream that pierced his heart like a knife. It was his wife. He began to shake her, shouting:

"What is it? What's happened to you?"

His wife lay speechless, trembling in every nerve of her body. He sprinkled water on her until she came back to life, when she whispered:

92

"We have lost our beloved son. He's gone. He has fallen on his back from a high road into a deep ditch, and is lying there, drenched in his own blood . . . his arms are apart, his feet above his head. . . ."

Nerimas tried to calm her: it was only a dream, and a dream always had a hidden meaning, if any at all. Mrs. Rimas came to console her, but the hearts of both neighbors were paralyzed, and trembled like captured sparrows. The autumn sky of Lithuania grew dark—and dark the whole village of Augštaičiai. All sensed the approach of a misfortune—they prayed; but this time, somehow, they felt that nothing could help them.

And nothing did. One day a postcard came to the village, again addressed as before: To Nerimas and Rimas, Augštaičiai, Kaunas Government. It was crumpled, dirty, almost washed out, soaked through not with water but with something thicker. Blood! . . . Everyone recognized it.

The message was brief:

"Pray for us. Rimas. Nerimas."

Below it were a few lines added by a nurse:

"This was found in Rimas's pocket. Nerimas was killed instantly on the highway back from Prussia. Rimas was wounded the same day and died in the hospital. Both heroes have been awarded the Cross of St. George which is given only to officers. May they rest in eternal peace!"

With this terrible document in his hand, Nerimas walked straight to Rimas himself—for the first time in nearly thirty years. Rimas saw his neighbor's pale face from a distance, saw that he was carrying something small in his hand and approaching him with uplifted eyes. Without a word he handed the card to Rimas, who took it in both hands, touched it with his fingers—and understood:

"Blood!" he screamed, staring wildly at Nerimas.

"Dead. . . . Both . . ." hoarsely answered Nerimas.

And the two men began to roar—there is no other way to describe the sound of their grief; never having shed a tear, they did not even know how to cry. They passed the bloody document of their children back and forth, as if they wanted to take it away from each other. But sound itself issued out of their throats almost without touching the vocal cords. They were not crying, but deep within their hearts something grasped them with an iron grip and made them roar.

Their families finally separated them, led each to his bed, and made them lie still. They fell silent, and seemed to pay no more attention to the others who had now begun to scream hysterically in a terrible way.

But at last even this came to an end.

And again the Rimases and Nerimases rode to church together; again they asked for joint obsequies "for eternal peace of the souls of Rimas and Nerimas." But now they rode in three wagons: Mrs. Nerimas with her children, Mrs. Rimas with hers, and Rimas and Nerimas together. They hummed softly, now and then wiping away a tear, and all their old hatred and relentless competition seemed to have vanished forever.

Alas, the war! What disasters and heartaches it brings! And how many hearts it cleanses and purifies. . . .

1915

The Misfit

Translated by Algirdas Landsbergis

THERE HAD NEVER been such a hot spell; even dusk brought no relief. Men and beasts dragged their feet, feeling barely alive. The grasshoppers alone kept showing how alive they were; their liveliness even seemed to be increasing as the draught grew worse. And who had provided them with gadgets, sharper than awls, to pierce men's ears? Yet the piercing and pricking of the insects brought no pain. It only made one dizzy and awakened a longing for summer. But there was no time for dreaming in the midst of the busy season.

"The bloody bugs, how come they don't dry to dust," our hired man was muttering as he entered the gate and tipped his cap before the tall wooden cross. He was passing a dense guelder-rose bush from which the grasshoppers seemed to be teasing the poor workmen.

It was already dark inside the cottage. In summertime, when days are long and nights short, lighting a lamp seemed indecent. Eating could be done in twilight and the light of the kerosene lamp could only disturb the sleepy weariness that seizes a poorly nourished body after its physical exertion of the day. Their meal finished, the men could hardly lift their hands to make the sign of the cross and, ghostlike, drag their feet to their flea traps for a deathlike sleep.

Three horses, their heads hanging listlessly, stood tied to an osier in the middle of the yard. Their paunches were empty and the way they were behaving suggested that they were hungry. The horses dozed as they waited in vain for someone to lead them out to pasture.

"Eh, what's going on?" the master, my father, realized belatedly. "Who'll take the horses to the pasture, now?"

It was not the thing for him to do, the man in charge with a family of at least ten. The women had already slunk into their storehouses and bolted their doors tightly.

My elder brother was silent. He seemed to be totally vanquished by work although he was still rolling a cigarette, having collapsed on the bench on the way to his bed.

The hired man got the message. "It's up to me, of course. Who else? One verst there another back, and it's midnight. And then getting up at four with the sun just beginning to rise—and fifteen hours of work. How can a man survive?"

He began putting his arm into the narrow sleeve of his jacket although he did not need it in such heat. "Do as you think best, Master, but I refuse to tend horses during summer harvest time."

It was true. One simply could not use a hired man for such purposes. Father was silent. He was evidently going to ride the horses himself.

I was still half-awake, although sleepiness and fatigue had overcome me. I enjoyed listening to the grasshoppers and watching the poor workmen and sympathizing with them.

"Daddy, please let me take a night ride, at least once. I'll sleep until breakfast."

I assumed that my father would not allow me to do this. I was not even allowed to tend the cattle during the day. I was the youngest and they pampered me and hired a shepherdess so I would not have to do any herding.

I was nearly eleven and was quick as a pepper although small and frail as a cricket. I had already managed to roll myself upon a horse when barefooted. To accomplish this, I needed to use the big toe of my left foot. I would push myself off from the horse's knee where, as luck would have it, there was a bump; then, mercilessly tearing at the mane, I would finally mount the animal. The horse suffered patiently through all these exertions and then obeyed as I rode, even when I would force him, through beating, to pretend that he was rushing into an all-out gallop. The "gallop" of the old creature was more like an aged crone's dance if anything, but it was enough for me; I prided myself about having galloped and was sufficiently excited by it.

Father contemplated my offer a while, took a large whiff of tobacco, looked at his littlest one across his shoulder and, with considerable contentment, said, "Well, why don't you ride for the night? And what do you lack to be a true night rider? You can hobble them, you can take off their halters. And at night, we've got the horseherd. In the morning, one of the older ones will help you manage."

I leaped with joy and boasted like a grownup, "That's small stuff, hobbling and halters . . . and I'll ride back properly."

What pleased me especially was that my mother did not hear any of the plan, for the next day I would be able to tell her about everything after it had happened! This meant that, for the first time, I would appear to her as a capable participant in farm work.

All three men felt a surge of joy, too, knowing that their life would now be easier. The disgruntled hired man suddenly became very co-operative and hurried to untie the horses. My older brother immediately snatched a huge fur coat and threw it over the horse, telling me in a consoling voice, "Here, bundle yourself up from head to toe like a little caterpillar; you'll sleep in a bed that's warm as a dumpling!" Then he flung me on the horse as though I were a sheaf of wheat.

I spread my legs wide and stretched out my arms like a gingerbread man. "Giddyap!" I shouted excitedly in my thin boyish voice and swept the horse-lock over their three backs.

The horses burst into a speedy trot, but I did not stop whipping them since I wanted them to gallop. I yelled and screamed so that the entire village could see me riding out that night. But the villagers did not see me since everybody was in bed, sleeping. The night herdsmen had all ridden out already, and even the dogs failed to do me honor. Not a single one of them barked at me from in front of the granaries. They must have assumed that one of their own was making all this noise.

The horses began trotting lazily as usual, but under the whip they broke into the gallop I desired. When we made the turn past Pečiūra's cottage, the last one in the village, they whinnied, as if in agreement, to a drove of horses dimly outlined in the distance, and showed that they could gallop properly.

For the first time, I realized with astonishment how great the difference between forced and voluntary labor was. The horses were giving all they had, even flattening themselves to the ground, as the saying here goes. They seemed to have grown smaller and the earth appeared to be closer to my feet. Hopping off would have been a very easy thing to do. But there was no time for that. The wind was rushing past my ears. The manes of the horses' necks, stretched in a cranelike fashion, spread out along their withers. The hair of their flying tails whistled like a whip. All at once, I became frightened. "Steady, horses, steady . . ." I muttered, nearly choking on my words. But they did not listen to me any longer. There was no more time to pull in the reins—I had to hold on to my horse's mane with both hands because my legs were hardly touching the animal's flanks and I was almost propelled into the air. If only I hadn't taken that coat! With its fur side out, it was sliding up and down on the slippery hair of the horse, and I could hardly hold it down with my legs.

"I'll fall . . . I'll kill myself. . . ." The thought terrified me and I did not even realize that I was squealing like a piglet.

A narrow bridge over a muddy stream loomed in the darkness ahead. It was laid over with loose boards that were wide enough for a one-horse carriage on a very straight course. The boards rattled like organ keys when the organist is giving them a nimble workout during mass, and they tended to tip over. It was possible to cross the bridge with a pair of horses if they pressed their flanks closely together. But with *three* horses, one had to wade through the stream.

My three chargers never stopped to give the matter a thought. In their wildness, they were probably not inclined to do any thinking at all, the only thing on their minds being how to reach that distant drove of horses. The boards thundered from their heavy hooves, and then the outside horse splashed into the stream, the middle one stumbled on a protruding board, and the animal I was riding fairly jumped across the bridge. I did not fall off, however, and I completed the ride to the edge of the marsh with two horses.

As we approached a group of horses which stood slightly apart from the rest of the herd, my mounts whinnied again. The other horses neighed in friendly response, and suddenly we came to a stop beside a man who was kneeling in the soggy grass. He had just about finished hobbling the last of them.

"What kind of a witch has come flying here with such thunder and squealing?" he asked, deeply curious.

I was still glued to the horse and felt half alive and half dead. Frightened and swooning, I clutched the animal's mane spasmodically and my tense fingers would not let it go.

"Who's here? Could that be Juzukas?" the man asked, coming closer. "Why did you go out riding? Come on, get off that horse! Where are your hobbles?" he asked as he eased me off the horse by my armpits.

There were no hobbles in my hands, no cap on my head, no fur coat on the horse, and the outside horse was still missing. In the next instant, however, it came snorting by, all covered with mud.

"Dashing . . . everything got scattered . . ." I started muttering, my jaws feeling as if they were locked stiffly in place.

The night herdsman understood. "Let them graze un-

99

hobbled for awhile," he said. "We'll go and gather your things."

That was not difficult. I knew the route I had taken. We found the things scattered on both sides of the stream. Back at the meadow, we hobbled the horses, found a dry place to sit down and started chatting.

Or, rather, I did all the talking, breathing nervously into my neighbor's ear about the terrors and dangers I had just experienced.

Although I exaggerated the dangers, I was truly convinced that if I had fallen off the horse my body would have broken to pieces, or, if I had slipped off the bridge with my horses, my back or spine would have cracked on the spot. It had seemed to me that each jump of the horse I was riding dealt a blow to my chest, pressed as it was against the animal's back. My chest still felt sore and I reclined on my side in order to rest and, if possible, to elicit more sympathy from my audience.

Pečiūra's Peleksas believed everything I said and managed to calm me down. He praised me for not falling off the horse and said it was time for both of us to go to sleep.

By now the other herdsmen had finished their work. Some were stretched out on the ground, their heads covered with short jackets to get quick warmth from their own hot breath. Their bare feet had been left unprotected, and they curled them under trying to get them to fit beneath the cover. But soon the feet would slide into the cold air again. Misery's own children they were, these men, like savages without roofs of their own.

Others continued to talk. Their speech was short—a few words here and there. Mostly, they kept turning and stomping their feet like dogs who turn and twist until they finally settle down on bare ground.

I was met with contemptuous smiles. The chief horse tender, bundled in "two's," which meant a woolen overcoat stuffed into a furcoat, and with his belt tightened to the limit, seemed to be prepared to drive to the forest instead

100

of being on a night watch. A thick sweater reached above his ears. All of this was in anticipation that the warmth of the late evening would give way to cold for a couple of hours before sunrise.

"Come now, they wouldn't be sending us such a horse tender for the night. Just the right fellow to guard us from thieves and wolves. . . ."

"And what would you do here? . . . Why should you get your wages if we need another watchman?" Peleksas growled. The horse tender shut his mouth and plunged into the darkness to check the horses.

I was expecting those who were still awake to surround me and question me in awed and fearful voices as to how I had managed to get there at full gallop without losing my head. But nobody asked me anything; for them, galloping and bouncing on a horse's back was quite an ordinary affair. So I started telling the story myself, without being asked. Yet even this made very little impression on them. The only thing that interested them a little was the fact that one of my horses had fallen into the stream.

"How come his weight did not pull down the others?" They asked me.

"Luckily, the harness was tied loosely around his neck and he slipped out of it."

"Some luck. . . . You'd have been as handsome as your horse!"

It seemed that the whole story would simply end there. But it really had only begun.

"What kind of fakery is this? Our gray mare has become dapple-gray!" The words greeted me as I rode into the yard.

"Was she stuck in the mud somewhere? Did you have to pull her out?"

I did not answer—making matters worse. The entire village was already buzzing with rumors of how I had drowned my horses in the stream and lost my head into the bargain.

People started coming and inquiring, while I snored

101

peacefully in a warm bed in the drawing room until it was almost lunch time.

The farm hands' lunch was brought to the field. I did not see them. In the afternoon, my mother kept glancing through the window and, having noticed Peleksas passing by, invited him inside. She made him sit in the place of honor and brought him a heaping saucer of buttered cream—twice as much as the saucer was meant to hold. She asked me to help him finish it. We ate and ate but more than half was still left. I was full and Peleksas shied away from eating too much in someone else's home. What would people think? Yet for a healthy, strapping fellow such as he was, a whole pitcherful would have come in handy!

Mother kept urging Peleksas to eat and was constantly nudging him, lifting his hand toward the saucer of cream as if he were paralyzed and inquiring about what had happened to me during the night.

"Oh, nothing. The horses made their run and the one on the outside slipped off the bridge. Nothing else, Auntie."

"And Peleksas helped me gather up the scattered things. Then he helped me ride back."

"Thanks to God for such an end! And here, people were concocting all kinds of stories. My son wouldn't tell me anything when he came riding home. . . . Well, you know he wants to tend the horses at night, but he's still a cricket—not big enough to catch a horse and too small to hobble it. You, Peleksas dear, you are a grown-up and steady lad. Couldn't you take our boy around with you when the others may need his help, at least for the busy season? They get tired, you know. How can they go on with their drudgery without sleep! And our Juzukas can get his sleep during the day, when he comes back."

"Will do," Peleksas replied and, having kissed my mother's hand, he started for the door. He was opening it when my mother caught up with him and stuffed a sizable chunk of her special barley bread into his pocket. "I'll send more of that to the field," she promised, raising her fore-finger in a conspiratory gesture.

Peleksas did not reply, as if he was unaware of the bread being slipped into his pocket or of the message that went with it. After taking several steps, however, he pinched off some of the soft middle of the bread with two fingers and, finding it delicious, started breaking off larger pieces. By the time he had entered his own yard, all the bread in his pocket was gone.

Peleksas had become very kindly disposed and was impressed that such a grand housewife had showered him with hospitality and promised him more tasty treats. But he began to feel something like a bribed man.

In our parts, if a neighbor shows you hospitality, it amounts to your borrowing from him; you have to pay him back in kind or reciprocate in some other way unless you want him to think badly of you.

Such had been the circumstances which had brought me and Peleksas together. We made for an odd couple, though. He was eighteen or nineteen—and I was not yet eleven.

II

We were the last family on the slope; Pečiūra's farm was the last one on the hill. We could never get together with this, our most distant neighbor. During the summer there was no time, and during the rest of the year the street was impassable. One could have tried to get there past the barns, but the high fences of the gardens provided formidable obstacles. And to top all that, uncle Pečiūra, Peleksas father, was a man who struck terror into our hearts.

He was handsome to look at, of medium height, clear-faced and endowed with a nose that sported a little aristocratic hump. His children were even handsomer. Fair-haired, they had such light complexions that even during the summer they did not get the faintest shade of tan. There were so

103

many red cheeks in the family that, as someone said, you could shave at night if they were around. This saying was aimed mainly at the Pečiūra girls because what fellow would stare at other fellows, especially in the darkness! Pečiūra's brood was so large that people in the village could barely remember the older children who had grown up and left home. But there were still plenty of them left at home. Peleksas was the youngest of them and almost a man himself. Meanwhile, Uncle Pečiūra was still in his middle years and had not even started to turn gray yet, as if he was ready to produce twice as many more offspring. However, he had too many worries about his brood already: to find husbands for his daughters, to marry certain sons to farm heiresses, to buy farms for others, to buy a farm for still others. And there was only so much property.

Night after night, Pečiūra would lie in bed without being able to fall asleep. Hands seemed constantly to be reaching out to him, demanding: for me, and for me, and for me! Uncle Pečiūra would turn on his side angrily and spit out his usual comment through his teeth: "May a bolt from the blue take care of you right now!" But even that did not help. His worries about how he could assure a good, which for him meant a rich, future for all his children simply refused to disappear.

This may have been the reason why Uncle Pečiūra became crafty and sly (unless he was born that way). His children were also sly, crafty and conniving, following in their father's footsteps. However, they were all loyal to their family and to the village.

Pečiūra's farmstead sprawled on the richest soil of the village. It was loam: not the red, sour variety, but the light-red loam that resembles wheaten dough because it has been mixed with a little sand.

Apple trees had a special fondness for that loam. Planted on a slope by Pečiūra himself, these trees "went crazy," according to the old saying, as they burst forth in ever new branches and foliage. Their leaves were almost as big as a man's palm, and the apples themselves seemed to have been molded by craftsmen from the purest wax. White with a shade of pink, they were unbelievably fair and completely spotless. And they were as huge as a sturdy man's fist.

The orchard was long and had at least three dozen trees in it. It would have been quite expensive to build a good fence around it, so all that surrounded it was a horizontal fence to protect it from animals since the enclosure for the cattle of the entire village was right next to it. As for people, anyone could easily have entered the orchard and taken his fill. Nevertheless, no thief, large or small, was ever known to have dared step across Pečiūra's fence, night or day. If some young pranksters would have ever thrown each other's caps into Pečiūra's orchard, they would probably have given them up rather than trying to jump over the fence, such terror had the frightening Pečiūra struck in the hearts of the young of the village by his guarded malice and watchfulness.

No one could imagine Pečiūra's drawing room, which faced the orchard, without Pečiūra himself standing behind the window. And even if he happened to be absent from the window, one envisioned him there or imagined he could see his face in the glass. Pečiūra was guarding his orchard. And that gave rise to a strange image of a huge eye—Pečiūra's eye—inside the glass—as large as that "eye of Providence" painted on covered posts by the wayside to remind everyone that God is watchful and alert, that He sees everything, no matter how one might try to hide it, and that He instantly administers severe punishment for any evil deed. The people of the village no doubt applied the idea of God's Providence to Pečiūra's watchfulness over his orchard and all his fields.

Pečiūra's homestead seemed to have been built especially for him, the keen watchman. The only place one could not really see from his farmhouse was the village itself, which was dense with trees. Pečiūra had a perfect view of the three other directions whenever he wished it: He could see

105

whether his horses and cattle were properly tended, whether
the boys had let the geese in their care wander into the
summer corn, or whether the swineherds had fallen asleep
and let the pigs loose to root up the meadows. The fact
that the shepherds and herdsmen were watchful and cau-
tious was due mainly to Pečiūra's ability to observe and his
readiness to grab the wrongdoer by the collar promptly,
throw him down and give him a merciless beating with that
well-known stick which, although not thick, was by no
means a mere rod. The stick was not a bone-breaker but,
pliant as it was, it could wind itself around the body contours
of the object of Pečiūra's wrath in order to inflict more pain.

Uncle Pečiūra never beat anyone, large or small, outside
his own family. He lived in peace with his neighbors, without any squabbles or quarrels; he would attend their chris-
tenings and funerals and would invite them to his. As for
his shepherd boys, he would frequently present them with
luscious apples, reserving the biggest one for the naughtiest
boy, saying: "Watch my little orchard, so that nobody will do
any harm to it. Some ignorant dolt will want to pluck one
apple only but in his fear and haste, he'll break a whole
branch. It won't do him any good but it will do a lot of
damage to the orchard: There will be ten apples less next
year. Besides, never you mind, I see and punish everyone
who deserves it, so you can tell others about this!"

The shepherd boys melted with fear as Pečiūra spoke.
And the most ruthless poacher of gardens and orchards
would wave his finger in front of the noses of the children
and threaten them: "Don't you dare put your foot on
Pečiūra's land!"

Uncle Pečiūra had never raised his hand against most
of his own people either. But all his children were afraid
of him and tried to oblige him, joining in the fun with
him whenever they felt that they would profit from it.
Peleksas alone, the youngest of the children, seemed to have
been hatched by some hobgoblin. He was totally unfit for
farm work or for village life.

Peleksas was not unpleasant to look at, however. He had his father's nose, although he was not of the usual fair complexion. As healthy as the other children in the family, he was nevertheless unusually lanky, and skinny as a sapling crowded in a thicket. He had black hair and handsome sky-blue eyes. Nobody saw their beauty, though: not his parents, nor his brothers and sisters, not even strangers. Peleksas never looked at anyone directly, only downward, at his feet, as if he were jealously guarding that treasure of his eyes. Even when he was sitting in a close circle of companions, he would direct the words of his answer (he rarely asked questions himself) to the bridle in his hands, to his pipe, his whittling, or to whatever he happened to be holding in his hands at the time: and never to the person who was addressing him. And his reply was always curt: He would twist his upper lip to the left and to the right, then pull his nose, in his father's manner, and stare at his knees again.

Nobody had ever seen Peleksas playing with other children, running with them across the silken meadow, turning somersaults or engaging in other childish fun. The people of the village noticed Peleksas only when he started taking the horses out for the night. But that had happened almost ten years before, and he had not changed any since then. Peleksas did not seem to fit anywhere else; he was Pečiūra's permanent horse tender and nothing more. He had become quite an expert at his trade but, as time passed, his father began to value him less and less, even as a horse tender.

Peleksas used to spend half of the year out-of-doors, most of the time reclined on his side at the foot of some hillock. His nights were spent turning and twisting on the same bare ground and in the same sweat-soaked fur coat. Such routine boredom had a soporific effect on Peleksas. He slept at night, whatever there was of it, and did not wake until breakfast. He could doze off instantly, at any time, and sleep as long as he was allowed to, as if he was in a state of lethargy. He slept and snored with such abandon, it was as though he wanted to make up for several days

107

of carousing. He would sleep undisturbed in a group whenever he was in a common tent, knowing that others would protect his horses from any harm.

His face would puff up from sleep, especially his upper lip. Then Peleksas would be ugly to behold, as though he had some kind of swelling disease or had been stung by bees. This would send the horse tenders into gales of mirth and mockery. They would dance around him and sing:

"What a lip, what a lip."

"Oh, that lip, lip, lip!"

Sometimes, having waited in vain for Peleksas to leave the tent and surmising that his lip had swollen to a proper size, they would tie his feet with a rein, attach a halter to the rein and, shouting encouragement to each other, would pull him out of the tent in the same manner that one drags wet sedges from a bog to a dry place: "Oh-ho-ho! Oh-ho-ho! Drag, drag! Pull, pull!"

Frightened and half-awake, Peleksas would fearfully grope for the ground, turning over and over until he realized what a team of horses was dragging him. He would not explode in anger or curse his tormentors or try to pick a fight with them. Peleksas never became involved in any quarrels. He would only loosen the bands on his feet, yawn broadly and, with studied indifference, stuff his pipe. As for his friends, they had no intention of abusing or denigrating him. He was quite a regular fellow, otherwise, brimming with brawn.

The men who tend the horses at night play their tricks on anyone, whether they are asleep or awake—even on those who resist being given a forcible ride by their feet! Some of these men would even try to creep into favor with Peleksas and ask him for a puff from his pipe. But he usually rebuffed such flatterers, and they had no choice but to go away and leave Peleksas alone.

Peleksas was always the last one to ride away and to ride back home. He was somewhat detached from the group and would become blanketed in a cloud of dust raised by those who rode in front of him. Yet he never stayed completely apart from the crowd. Even during herding, he would sit somewhat apart from the group although not far enough apart to miss any of their conversation. He did not drop out; he participated in the group despite his silence and his sham indifference. Nobody bothered to find out what Peleksas was thinking in his solitude; and nobody cared anything about what he felt, what things delighted him, or what he found disgusting.

It was the same situation at home. Silently, Peleksas would sit down at the table and, in silence, carry out his orders. He never quarreled with his parents or his brothers. Nevertheless, they all felt that Peleksas was not quite like the other members of the family; he was almost completely alien in his own home. He did not care about either the present or the future, about what he would do when he became a man or how his brothers and sisters would fare. He merely lived; and he lived not as a candle burns, but as a stick smolders. Peleksas was not a member of Pečiūra's farmstead or of the village—he was a misfit, that's all.

Old man Pečiūra worried about him, too. And his ire grew unchecked when Peleksas turned out to be neither farmer, nor craftsman, nor singer, nor even a party-going rake! He was neither fish nor fowl. And Pečiūra began to think that Peleksas alone obstructed his efforts to ensure a good future for all the members of his family. Things grew worse as time went on. The old man developed a passionate hatred for his youngest son. He felt like kicking him whenever he passed by. If he failed to do that, he looked for an excuse to find fault with him and give him a painful beating. After doing that, he would quiet down for a week. Then, again devoured by bitterness, he would look around, at home and in the fields, to see what Peleksas was doing. Finally, he would swoop like a buzzard to the edge of the marsh, knowing that he would find Peleksas asleep there, and would relieve himself of his anger by thrashing his son's hide. Peleksas was a nimble youth and whenever his father would surprise him unawares and start beating him painfully with his cane, he would slither like an adder trapped between his father's arms and legs. But the old man was also quite agile and would manage to seize some end of his son and beat him until his wrath was spent.

In the market, Pečiūra came upon a thin and flexible but strong cane, and started bargaining for it. A neighbor who happened to be passing by wondered why he needed such a cane. Was this not something young gentlemen carried on their idle walks? What farmers needed was a solid stick, good for attack and defense.

Pečiūra answered firmly, "Just the thing to thrash Peleksas with."

"What for?" the neighbor asked.

"Ah, he's a misfit, that's what for."

III

The following day, when I rode my team of three horses to the edge of the marsh, Peleksas had already let loose his three good horses and had returned to the dry land, the black patches of his wet knees indicating that he had shackled his team while kneeling in a wet spot. Seeing me, Peleksas seemed to perk up from head to toe. He stopped my horses by the bridle and wanted to help me down, but this touched my most sensitive spot and I slid down from my horse on my stomach without any help.

The two of us and our horses found ourselves some distance from the others, as usual. Later, we joined the group again. Meanwhile, I considered it my duty to remind Peleksas that he had been bribed by my family and was therefore like a servant or slave.

"My mother gave you a treat yesterday and I promised to give you wheaten bread; so you'll help me gather my horses tomorrow!"

"Will do," Peleksas agreed as he removed the headstalls

110

of the bridles and threw a handful of them at me. They had to be arranged neatly, as one arranges a long rope, and be tied with one headstall to prevent them from being scattered all over the place and lost in a pile of others. When the herders went to sleep, they put them beside, or even under, their heads.

We found a crowd of night herders getting ready to go to sleep. They were arguing about the arrangement; nobody wanted to be situated at the edge of the group. And there was good reason for that: should a wolf or some other creature of the dark grab someone, who else would it be but the fellow at the end of the row?

"I won't lie down last—I won't. . . ." I seized Peleksas' hand fearfully.

"Don't scare yourself. There's nothing to be afraid of. There are no wolves or bears here and no forests where they could live. And as for the ghosts, they're hiding inside the castle mounds. You know what? Let's lie down by ourselves. We can use my coat as a sheet and yours as a blanket, and we'll be warm on all sides."

We did exactly that. One fellow immediately plopped himself down next to us, then another, and then another—and a latecomer was stuck at the edge. Thus, we solved the problem of positions for the night.

I found myself at Peleksas' side, just as I had, long ago, found myself at my mother's side in a feather bed. I felt warm and happy. I clasped Peleksas' neck and hugged him and he tucked me in carefully to make certain I would not freeze because of some little gap in the coverings.

We woke up at sunrise and I lifted the edge of the fur coat and peeked out. The whole world glimmered and glowed in joyous sunlight. It was getting warmer and the soil was sweating in big dew drops and then drying instantly. It would be a clear day. I knew that I should get up but this was not easy to do at sunrise. At that hour of day, most living creatures are drowned in sleep and find it virtually impossible to rouse themselves. Even if one found

111

a real wolf at one's side, one would simply offer the animal an opportunity to join in the slumber.

When I awakened for the second time, I felt like a caterpillar wrapped in a huge fur coat, while Peleksas was chasing the horses wearing only his shirt! He had taken pity on me and had not pulled out his two coats from under me. Rather than disturb me, he risked freezing in his shirt. I understood that and felt that it was improper for me to take such advantage of my friend's thoughtfulness.

"Peleksas, you'll freeze to death. Why don't you get your clothes?" I asked.

"The sun will warm me. Look, it's rising higher and higher—sending more and more rays and more and more warmth. After a little while, it will be so warm we'll have to take a dip somewhere."

We sat down together on the slope. I could not recognize Peleksas. He was gazing around, his eyes wide open, fixing them now and then on some spot. I saw, for the first time, what beautiful eyes he had. With those sky-blue eyes that expressed such joy and longing, he now looked straight at me. I was even more astonished by Peleksas' unexpected loquacity.

"Juozas, dear, wouldn't you like to cross all the marshes now and get to the bluff of the highest valley to watch the sunrise from there?"

"No. What good would that do?"

"But I would like to. And then go from that peak through other marshes to that distant hill. . . ."

"And what will you find there?" I asked.

"It's far away . . . and then even farther. To go and go . . . very far . . . all by myself along nice dry highways—or, even better, not along the highways but across the hills and meadows and along the rivers. . . ."

"And what for?"

"Just like that—without worry or fear of being followed. . . . And that's what I'll do when I put my mind to it."

"And your father? He'll snoop and search and run

112

around and scream. . . . And when he finds you, he'll give you a licking." As I spoke, I was suddenly seized with fear that his father would start beating a lad who had turned out to be so adult and so handsome.

Peleksas did not answer at first. He was still not sure about his plans.

"I need to know," he said finally, "to know a lot: who, where and how. Then, even my father won't find me. But how will I find out if I don't go to these places?"

"I've already finished half of my primary schooling," I bragged. "And I got on the honor roll, too!"

"But what do you know about our land?" Peleksas asked with intense curiosity.

"Well, nothing, really. I read and write and do arithmetic . . . and I'm memorizing the catechism. That's about all."

In reality, I was as unschooled as the other children; just as Peleksas was, too.

"But my father didn't teach me anything," he said. "He taught everybody to read except me."

"Why?"

"How do I know? He doesn't want me to be like the others or like him. He sleeps as long as he wants to, but he forbids me to do the same. Instead, he beats me, saying that sleep is bad for me. He puffs his pipe whenever he feels like it and as much as his heart desires but he forbids me to smoke and he beats me again, saying it's bad for me. Whatever's bad for me seems to be good for him. He downs a glass or two during holidays, but he scolds others who drink. He's hellbent on making a profit, but if anybody else tries to do the same, he calls him a Jew. I don't know what I should do—what's good and what's bad. Perhaps it's something I should decide myself."

We sat there for a long time after our conversation, gazing around at the beautiful countryside. Peleksas kept training his sights on more and more distant things, while I rejoiced in little things close to me. I found the greens alongside the marsh and the small meadows enormously pleasant. Here, I was comfortable and felt that I was myself. But when I gazed at that boundless horizon, I felt that I was nothing, a mere nothing. Peleksas evidently felt just the opposite.

It was Sunday and we lay for a long time in the sun, feeling warmer and better all the time. But Peleksas was restless. It seemed that he wanted to contribute something of his own to that harmony of summer. The violin or clarinet would have suited him well if he could have played it softly, as softly as if nature itself was making those sounds. But Peleksas was incapable of that, either.

"You know what? You stay here alone (it was as if he did not see the others who were a short distance away), look after the horses and I'll run home and bring back some breakfast for us."

"Why should you go? We'll have to be returning home soon anyway and a good breakfast will be waiting for us."

"No—definitely not! I'd rather stay here." With that, he dashed off on his long legs and was back in half an hour. He was carrying a pile of soft rye pancakes wrapped in a white kerchief, and a small jar of butter.

We were naturally quite hungry. Nevertheless, I felt somewhat uneasy. "Peleksas," I asked, "did my mother give you all this?"

"No, she didn't see me," he replied.

"How did you get it, then?"

"I came in from the garden, past the barn."

I would never have dared to help myself to the pancakes, not to mention the butter, without having first asked my mother. But Peleksas did not share my scruples.

"Here, eat!" he said, offering me the tasty pancakes and butter. Overcome by hunger, I took some and enjoyed them, even though I was aware of my participation in the theft.

Peleksas felt happier with every minute. He ate with relish, scooping the butter and swallowing the soft pancakes

114

without bothering to chew them. He twisted his mouth in all kinds of ways, deeply inhaling through his nose as he ate.

Having finished our meal, we got our horses together and rode home . . . to breakfast. I just couldn't eat any more, and everybody wondered why. But I would not explain. I felt no scruples any longer.

Why did Peleksas do it? I think that probably he had to—that he could not help doing it. He simply had to treat himself.

Suddenly, Peleksas changed completely. He began looking straight into other people's eyes—not only mine—and sometimes, out of the blue and without being asked, he would say, "Your mother gave me a treat. . . ."

Peleksas watched over me like a nursemaid. And he had no secrets from me. I don't recall how long this juvenile idyll lasted; I only remember how it ended—and I shall never forget it.

Greed had taught us, children and grownups alike, to snatch as much as we could from the common holdings. The pasture, for example, was for common use. But the especially solicitous tenders fed their horses by hand. They would take a quick look around and then lead their horses to where they thought the grass was more abundant—as though the horses themselves did not know where the grazing was best! Moreover, the horse tenders actually interfered with the grazing by their continuous criss-crossing from one spot to another.

Soon this manifestation of greed became infectuous, and everybody started doing the same thing, including myself. Peleksas was the only one who refused to adopt the practice. And, to tell the truth, his horses were better fed than the rest.

Once, when the horses were grazing contentedly and Peleksas was snoring on a hillock, Uncle Pečiūra suddenly emerged out of nowhere and started beating Peleksas for neglecting his duties. He struck him wildly and with such fury that we became nauseated. It was then that we started

115

hating Pečiūra with all our hearts and stopped calling him "Uncle." Only our terror of him prevented us from slinging mud at him.

Another time, Peleksas was busy at the foot of a hillock, making a wooden form for the bottom part of a pipe bowl which he was eventually going to cast from tin. I am sure that he devised it himself, since nobody could have shown it to him. He brought a fragment of glass to smelt the tin, lit a fire and was about to complete the carving of his form without releasing his pipe from his mouth. We were sitting around and following with greatest interest what would result from Peleksas' craftsmanship. So we did not notice Pečiūra again emerging right next to us, as if he had come out of a hole in the ground. He wrenched the pipe from Peleksas' teeth and then the unfinished one from his hands and broke both to pieces. Then he started thrashing the craftsman with his cane for puffing "that stinking pipe." "Oaf and whippersnapper," he called Peleksas. "Hell and damnation!"

That incident was the final straw, and Pečiūra's reputation became extinguished in our eyes. We all sympathized deeply with our friend and were, at the same time, astounded by his failure to avoid his father's blows.

Peleksas remained sitting although he had been struck at least five times in the same place on his back. His face completely expressionless, he just stared with his big eyes at the beastly rage of his father and refused to budge. The blank look on his face was terrifying to behold, and Peleksas' father noticed it, too. He spat angrily on the ground, flung out one more thunderous curse and left for home in a hurry.

After that time, Peleksas stopped looking directly at people again. He stopped all his activity and seemed to be interested only in sleep. He would cover his head only and sleep day and night—or perhaps he was only pretending to be asleep because he was not interested in looking at the world any longer. And nobody ever thought of mocking him for his continual sleeping or of playing tricks on him.

We also stopped sleeping apart from the others. Peleksas began walking around the horses at night and, later on, he would disappear completely. The sleeping men did not notice his absence, however. Only the old herdsman was aware of it and later informed on him.

Peleksas started stinking of brandy and old Pečiūra began to complain that his things were disappearing. Everybody wondered how Pečiūra could miss such doings under his very nose. Pečiūra had noticed the change in Peleksas and followed him. With the help of some other men, he seized a Jew who was selling brandy secretly. They found Pečiūra's missing objects in the man's place and forced him to divulge who had brought them. The Jew betrayed Peleksas.

Pečiūra roared back home with the men and, with their help, brought in reins, horse collars, a plank and sticks. Peleksas, his face as white as a linen cloth, was sitting by the stove. Nobody showed him any sympathy and even his own mother was aloof.

"Well, get him!" Pečiūra screamed, and two men seized Peleksas.

Peleksas did not resist. He merely looked around with his ghastly eyes and warned the neighbors, "If you're going to beat me, then beat me to death. Otherwise, I won't forgive you. First, I'll fry my father alive in his own house; and then I'll get to you. Father, I stole because I wanted to revenge myself. I decided to pay you evil for evil. All my life, you've tortured me. If I'm a thief, then you're *all thieves:* you, and you, and you, and your sons. Search the Jew's place; you'll find more stuff there. . . . Where will you start, you animals . . . ?"

Peleksas' words sent his father into a frenzy. The neighbors became infuriated, also. They beat Peleksas with all their strength but stopped short of torturing him. And they never saw him again. He vanished, leaving the villagers in a terrible fear.

"He'll burn us down, the freak!" Pečiūra worried. So did the neighbors, all of whom felt guilty.

"Why did *we* have to get involved? Peleksas stole from Pečiūra and Pečiūra should have meted out the punishment. Did Peleksas harm *us* in any way?"

For a while, the villagers scarcely slept at all. Two watchmen made the rounds each night and would raise an alarm sometimes, but in vain. Peleksas never appeared again. The summer passed and then fall and winter went by.

In the spring, rumors reached the village that, in some distant village, a horse thief had been caught and killed and that his murderers were now in jail. The dead thief was a certain Peleksas Pečiūra, a vagabond without any documents. Previously, he had been seen loitering in several other districts.

The village thanked God for the disappearance of the spectre. Pečiūra, who always used to complain: "What a son has God given to me; may hell take him," was suddenly silent.

One Sunday, Pečiūra's wife came home from church where she had bought a Mass for Peleksas' soul. As she was handing the money to the priest in church, she wept bitterly and told him the whole story, between sobs. The priest listened to her but did not offer a single word of consolation.

"Let us pray," he said. "As for Peleksas, you, his own parents, ruined him yourselves. You saw that he could not be a land tiller, so you should have taught him some craft or sent him to school so that he could have become a normal human being."

When the Pečiūras went to bed that night and the old man exploded in his usual manner about his wife being so jumpy and restless, she bluntly told him, "The priest says that we, Peleksas' parents, have destroyed our son." And she repeated the conversation.

Pečiūra cursed the priest but he, too, spent the night turning and tossing without being able to sleep. He never complained to anybody about Peleksas again. However, he did not go to the place where his son had died, nor did he confront Peleksas' murderers.

When I heard all that had happened, I timidly pulled my mother aside and asked, "Have you heard . . . that Peleksas was murdered?"

"Yes, I heard," she replied sadly. "May he rest in eternal peace. He never harmed us in any way."

"He never harmed anyone . . ." I began. "If you only knew what a good person he was, how gentle. . . ." I burst into tears, unable to continue. And mine were probably the only tears that were shed for the misfit Peleksas.

1929

Aleksiukas' Father and Mother

Translated by Danguolė Sealey

IN THE TAUČIUS HOUSEHOLD, which was no less than ten members strong, Aleksiukas, the youngest, was the most loved and cherished. Only his father did not caress him, kiss him, or play with him. Aleksiukas thought himself indeed fortunate, when on rare occasions he was taken upon the paternal knee. . . . Yet, despite this apparent coldness, Aleksiukas knew that in his own way no one loved him as much as his father.

How many times during the day did his father open the kitchen door and glance at Aleksiukas crouched in a corner over his playthings?

His father's glance made Aleksiukas tremble with happiness, yet he did not rush on all fours to his father, as he did to his mother; he merely left his toys alone and gazed at the tranquil face. . . . Or, overcome by this pure emotion, he would throw himself on the cushion, but continue to watch his father stealthily and with secret delight.

Aleksiukas' father, Taučius, was of low build—he had powerful shoulders, a forehead like a dome, and greying hair.

He trimmed his moustache more severely than was the custom of his day, and the mere tuft on his upper lip both protected his garments from snuff and lent to his face a mild and harmless air.

He was serious, yet no one feared him: neither fowls nor beasts, nor the children who were hired to look after the

121

herd. It was difficult to praise him or to speak ill of him, for Taučius was an unobtrusive man, who supported his large family by his own toil and who did not seek help.

He had never learned to swear, and anyone who had the misfortune to provoke him heard no stronger word than "rascal." When brought to the very end of his patience, he would grow visibly agitated, scold the culprits in a voice more loud than angry, and hasten immediately to his wife.

"Mama, what made them disobey me? The rascals!"

Then he would draw his snuffbox from his waistcoat pocket and take a substantial pinch. His eyes would close and an expression of contentment and mild resignation would at last spread over his face.

He was equally unable to rejoice aloud. Only when he heard a very funny story, indeed, would his lips move in a fleeting smile—but on perceiving it he would take snuff to calm himself.

Taučius always walked with an even gait—neither hurrying nor dawdling. He was never idle. Although he did not work in the fields any more, he still kept busy with the farm buildings. All day long he was on his feet around the barns and the storehouses; he helped to dry the hay and the flax, and to thresh the corn.

In wintertime he made implements for the farm—dressers, dowry chests, and wooden plates. He was a skillful craftsman. He fashioned everything for his own use, but could not be persuaded to work for money.

As he worked thus at a leisurely pace, shaping the wood with a plane or a chisel, Aleksiukas would sit with his chin propped on his fist, watching his father for hours in silence from the other side of the bench. Or he would lean against his father's thigh and amuse himself by playing with the wood-shavings.

From time to time, Taučius would set his work aside and reach into his waistcoat pocket for his snuffbox. He would give several smart taps on its birch lid before opening it, draw the aromatic powder together, and take a generous pinch with the tips of his fingers; taking a deep breath, he would draw in half of the pinch and hold back the remainder in readiness, his hand resting on his knee.

Sometimes, when he knew that Aleksiukas was watching him intently, he would hold out his fingertips towards the little boy in jest. But Aleksiukas knew that snuff was not for little boys, and his father's offer made him laugh more than anything later in life ever could.

Aleksiukas loved his father but avoided him, and for a long time he could not tell why. Later he realized that of all praiseworthy things that moved him, the most powerful was a man's full heart, rich in unexplored kindness. His silent father was full of mysteries like the bed of a still river; its depth might conceal pearls and perhaps thorns, too. . . .

✔ ✔ ✔

It was a warm and beautiful summer's day. Taučius was standing on the porch of the storehouse in his shirtsleeves, sharpening a scythe. Aleksiukas, likewise in shirtsleeves, was watching his father as he always did. The little boy listened entranced to the even blows of the hammer, and looked as though he could listen thus for a thousand years. . . . And no wonder: it was his father at work. Wherever Taučius went, Aleksiukas went, too.

Taučius finished sharpening his scythe; he bent down to examine the blade and made sure that the handle was firmly held in place. Then, after his manner, he took snuff; and when he had put away his snuffbox, he said, "Do you want an apple?"

For Aleksiukas an apple was scarcely a treat. He was the king of the orchard. But he wanted to keep his father at his side for as long as he could, and so he clapped his hands and chanted, "Yes, yes, yes. . . ."

Taučius rose slowly to his feet and began to search among the wood-shavings in the yard for a hazel-stick. When he had found one to his satisfaction he split one end of it carefully and thrust in a piece of wood to make a fork. If it was a light rod, Aleksiukas would carry it on his shoulder and walk solemnly in front of his father singing hymns, as though he were bearing a cross to the cemetery. If it was heavy, he would drag it along on the ground, sitting astride it, as if he were on a horse. They marched in procession to the "soft" apple tree.

On arriving in the orchard, they would place themselves in the full light of the sun and examine the tree very carefully to see if yet another apple had ripened to the color of pale wax. This time they caught a glimpse of a real beauty among the top branches. It was as big as Aleksiukas' two fists together! But unfortunately, the fork which Taučius held in his hand was too short to reach the fruit.

"Come here, Aleksiukas, I'll lift you on my shoulder, and you will hit the apple with the stick."

Aleksiukas seized the fork and raised it carefully. But when he let it drop in the direction of the coveted apple, the fork refused to obey him and fell just where it pleased; it brought down several green apples.

"Well, try once more."

Again Aleksiukas raised the fork, but now his hands were trembling and laughter bubbled inside him; and again the fork struck amiss. His lively chuckle disturbed the peace of the orchard. . . .

Taučius pretended to be cross and, as if upbraiding his assistant, planted Aleksiukas squarely on the ground.

"Why, you're not much of a workman. Look how many apples you've ruined, while trying to get the ripe one down."

"But what shall we do now?" asked the child with concern.

"I don't know," replied Taučius disdainfully and again reached for his snuffbox. The yellow apple gleamed and glistened at the top of the tree, as if it were poking gentle fun at the two people standing beneath it.

By now Aleksiukas felt that he must get the better of the apple, not so much to eat it as to overcome its stubborn opposition. He began to look around anxiously for better tools.

Suddenly he noticed the long bench standing under the sturdy willow-tree that spread like an umbrella in the middle of the yard; on fine evenings, the family ate their supper in its shade, when they came home from the fields.

With a great show of cleverness the little boy exclaimed, "Father, let me lift you up. . . ."

"Well, go on then," replied Taučius still with complete unconcern, as though the feat were quite possible.

Aleksiukas giggled and ran off into the yard. He turned the bench upside down. Then, walking backwards, he began to drag it laboriously into the orchard. He looked like an ant struggling with an enormous stick. Taučius pretended not to see his pathetic plight; taking some snuff with the tips of his fingers, he let his gaze wander among the tree-tops, as though he were counting the stars.

At last Aleksiukas reached the apple-tree. Taučius climbed up on the bench and deftly hooked the apple. He twisted the twig till it broke; the apple dived through the leaves and bounced at their feet, splitting its skin and oozing with juice.

Aleksiukas pounced on the apple like a hound on a wounded bird; he seized it in both fists and showed it to his father. He raised it high above his head, beaming with delight, and rolled it about in the palms of his hands.

Taučius climbed down from the bench and rested the stick against his shoulder; then he looked at his son and rummaged for his snuffbox.

"You must have the first bite, Father. Aleksiukas stretched his short arms as far as he could.

"Thank you, but I have no teeth left. . . ."

"Oh, but you have, you have. . . . Try with your big tooth," Aleksiukas pressed him.

Taučius could not resist such a forthright invitation. He accepted the apple gravely and placed a piece of it inside the corner of his mouth, while Aleksiukas watched him with hands clasped behind his back and head thrown back.

When he had eaten a little, Taučius returned the apple saying, "You have the rest."

"Oh, eat some more, Father, do eat some more! . . ."

Aleksiukas took the apple without enthusiasm, realizing with regret that the expedition to the orchard was now truly over, and that his father intended in all earnestness to return to the work he had interrupted.

Aleksiukas knew that in the whole world there had never been a better father than his.

*　　　*　　　*

Aleksiukas' mother was quite different from his father. It seemed as though some fate had brought them together so that each could complement the other.

Taučius was a man of few words; his wife spoke enough for them both. She was silent only when she slept. But even in her sleep she was restless and coughed nearly all the time. As long as she was on her feet, she was the life and soul of her household. The minute she wakened, she would hurry to get everyone else up and tell them what to do, although the work had already been decided upon and parcelled out by her husband the night before. She was always consumed with anxiety lest any time should be wasted, and in her zeal she would scold everyone, saying that they did not pay her the slightest heed. Or she would complain at great length how difficult it was to live with such a slow-going husband, or again she would recount aloud the tasks which awaited her now and later in the day. As long as anyone remained in the room, she would talk about the past; and when she was left by herself, she would sing hymns. And so it went on all day long. Even when she was ill, Mrs. Taučius would not cease talking, but was forever sending the other members of the family about their business, or quarreling with one or another of the housemaids.

Nor did her own tasks—which she never seemed to put aside—present any formidable obstacles to her voice. On the contrary, the harder she worked, the more and the louder she

126

talked. When her hands were busy, words seemed to flow from her like the humming sound from a spinning wheel.

She would talk as she ran out of the room; she would talk as she made the swill for the pigs; she would talk as she fed the calves, churned the butter, saw to the milk, the meat, and the sausages. For the most part this very abundant flow of words was directed at her son Aleksiukas; when the grown-ups had gone, there was no one else to talk to. And as soon as Aleksiukas was old enough to remember what she said, he learned from her by heart the full history of his father's and her own kinsfolk: of their sufferings, misfortunes, and joys; to say nothing of her personal past sorrows, present anxieties, heartbreaks, expectations, and forebodings.

As a result, Aleksiukas became convinced from the very start that his mother preserved order in the household by her talk alone. It seemed to him that if his mother should ever stop talking, urging them on, or ordering them about, everything would fall to pieces and collapse; and Heaven alone could tell what would become of them! So in his prayers he used to beg God earnestly, for the sake of their survival, to protect his mother, who was so diligent and conscientious, from all the evils that might befall her.

Mrs. Taučius' devotion to her family and her never-ending anxiety for their well-being were really boundless. Aleksiukas was a veritable martyr to her love. He was her last-born, her tenth child, a late and somewhat unexpected arrival, born when she was no less than 45 years old; and thus he had always seemed to her more of a toy bestowed in her old age than an ordinary baby. She kissed and fondled him almost continually. The small victim of her love had to attend to endless litanies of endearments in the course of the day. Surely there could not have been a better or a more loving mother in the whole world!

She also prayed just as fervently as she practiced her housekeeping and ruled her house. She said her prayers often, sometimes aloud and even in tears, subjecting herself utterly to the will of the Lord. At night, when she gave thanks for the blessings of the day, she would fall prostrate upon the ground, embracing it and kissing it devoutly, and address herself directly to the earth: "Black Earth, Holy Earth, I humbly kiss thee, I thank thee for bearing me, sustaining me, and giving me joy. . . ."

Such was the never-varying incantation with which she began her evening prayers.

Everywhere she recognized the special dispensation of Providence, the very Hand of God. For her, Nature was full of the Almighty Will. She would not suffer anyone to speak ill of the good earth; she would use only the purest water, drawn straight from the well, to put the fire out. She was deeply, even fanatically devout.

Since Mrs. Taučius was quite incapable of moderation in her work, her devotions, her gait, or her talk, but was always in a hurry, always anxious and flustered, she gave the impression of being nothing but a bundle of nerves. Her low stature increased her agility; her dark complexion and even darker hair suited her temperament.

Was she beautiful? Hardly. At fifty her face was prematurely lined; her eyes had a faded look; she was thin and flat-breasted. It was the effect not so much of old age as of ill-health and exhaustion. She had admittedly married into a family which did not work for the squire but paid rent in money instead; besides, her husband's brother was one of the bailiffs. Nevertheless, she had a clear recollection of physical pain and of famine; she had given birth to ten children and had buried five of them. These sorrows had been almost unbearable for a woman of her innate sensitivity; they broke her health and left their mark on her face and form. Not that it was of the least consequence to her family.

On weekdays, Aleksiukas' mother used to wear a short, homespun skirt and a jacket of the same material; she also wore a white linen blouse cut like a man's shirt, and a white linen apron. Usually she went about barefoot, for she said it was cumbersome to work or spin with shoes on. Around her neck there hung many scapulars, a large medallion of St. Dominic, and an equally large brass cross, which contained relics of the holy martyrs.

She also owned a "Sunday" skirt which was cut and pleated in hussar style. This garment meant as much to her as did her girlhood memories.

✓   ✓   ✓

It was Sunday. The sun had climbed a good distance in the sky, but the household was still asleep, except for the herdsman who had driven the cattle to pasture and one of the women who stood by the kitchen-range preparing breakfast.

Soon it was time for breakfast. It was bright and cheerful in the room. One by one the family appeared, spruce in their clean linen. The girls had not put their hair up yet, and came to table with it hanging down their shoulders.

"Time for breakfast, children. Heaven help us! Before we know where we are, our neighbors will be starting off for church!"

Mrs. Taučius was full of her usual impatience as she hurried them along, bustling about with a dish of warm, soft pancakes in one hand and a bowl of drippings in the other.

Taučius seated himself in the place of honor on the bench beneath the window, leaving room for his wife, even though she never sat still for two minutes together. On his left sat his oldest son and the hired men. His daughters seated themselves next to the maidservants on the moveable bench at the opposite side of the table. If some hungry passer-by happened to be invited to share the meal, he would be asked to sit with the women, too.

Each member of the family crossed himself in his own way, depending on the degree of his piety or hunger. Some did so slowly and devoutly; others rapidly, without any sense of reverence. Then they all reached into the dish with their fingers, and soon afterwards the room was filled with the loud smacking of lips. The pancakes were followed by a dish of meat and by oatmeal soup, which they took instead of tea, while their wooden spoons clattered noisily.

It was Aleksiukas, of course, who presided at table. He sat between his parents and was fed with the choicest bits.

Not that he felt in the least hungry, but all the same he liked to sit together with the others; he liked to watch them eating—to look at their faces, which became red and sweaty from the scalding broth—and to observe the thin spirals of steam rising from the plates. He liked the smell of pancakes, too; but, perhaps most of all, he liked to listen to the smacking of lips and to the sound of soup being swallowed.

"Look, the others are already on their way," exclaimed his mother in great agitation as one cart came rolling by along the road.

"We're always the last to set off! Always the last! Quick, harness the horses, otherwise we'll be late for Mass. Girls, come with me at once to the storehouse."

For Taučius, this was scarcely news. He knew that he would reach the church no later than the others; and so he rose to his feet without undue haste. The other men followed his example. All of them sat down again for a minute on the ends of the benches, and only after that did they start for the door with heavy, languid steps.

"Good heavens, how slow they are! You'd think they were half-dead already. . . ." Mrs. Taučius could scarcely bear to watch them.

Smarting with annoyance, she threw herself headlong through the door and called out after her, "Girls, come with me at once!"

Two of her daughters, with tears in their eyes, rushed after her and implored her: "Oh Mo-o-other, please don't put on your old-fashioned hussar skirt this time!"

"What nonsense you talk, you two geese!" she snapped, tossing her head as all three, talking heatedly among themselves, hurried straight to the storehouse where the dowry chests were kept.

And soon afterwards, when two dejected girlish faces reappeared outside the door of the storehouse, the maid-servant quickly cleared the table and wiped it down with a cloth. The daughters approached the house, each holding one end of something black, folded, and tied with ribbons and braid. Their mother walked solemnly behind them, as though she were following the canopy beneath which the Blessed Sacrament is carried during solemn processions.

They brought their burden into the room, spread it out on the table, untied all the ribbons (with their noses still in the air), and let loose the hundred pleats of a shiny black skirt. With great caution they removed all traces of lint and held up the skirt in their hands. It was a perfect garment.

1918

DATE DUE